D1011199

ROBINSON

ROBINSON

Christopher Petit

VIKING

VIKING
Published by the Penguin Group
Penguin Books USA Inc., 375 Hudson Street,
New York, New York 10014, U.S.A.
Penguin Books Ltd, 27 Wrights Lane,
London W8 5TZ, England
Penguin Books Australia Ltd, Ringwood,
Victoria, Australia
Penguin Books Canada Ltd, 10 Alcorn Avenue,
Toronto, Ontario, Canada M4V 3B2
Penguin Books (N.Z.) Ltd, 182-190 Wairau Road,
Auckland 10, New Zealand

Penguin Books Ltd, Registered Offices:
Harmondsworth, Middlesex, England

First American Edition
Published in 1994 by Viking Penguin,
a division of Penguin Books USA Inc.

1 3 5 7 9 10 8 6 4 2

PUBLISHER'S NOTE
This is a work of fiction. Names, characters, places and incidents either are the product
of the author's imagination or are used fictitiously, and any resemblance to actual persons,
living or dead, events, or locales is entirely coincidental.

Portions of this book first appeared as a short story entitled "Robinson" in *Granta*.

Two lines from *The Collected Poems of Weldon Kees* are reproduced by kind permission of
The University of Nebraska Press.

LIBRARY OF CONGRESS CATALOGING IN PUBLICATION DATA

Petit, Christopher
Robinson / Christopher Petit
p. cm.
ISBN 0-670-84925-1
I. Title.
PS3566.E7738R6   1994
813'.54—dc20   93-31578

Printed in the United States of America
Set in Garamond

BEFORE

Deep assignments run through all our
lives; there are no coincidences.

J. G. Ballard

Robinson alone at Longchamps, staring at the wall.

Weldon Kees, 'Aspects of Robinson'

THERE WAS SOMETHING vaguely familiar about Robinson. Long after we became friends I remembered I had seen him once before in a pub called the Angel, standing at the bar with another man. I had been struck by his air of persuasion and watched out of idle curiosity while waiting for a woman who was late. Robinson physically dominated the conversation. I thought he would overstep the mark, but his positioning was faultless. The other man nodded a lot and had on a dark jacket, I remember, because at one stage Robinson, without interrupting himself, leaned over and brushed something from the lapel.

Had I not subsequently met him I would have forgotten the incident (and did until much later anyway). Looking back, I remember his intimacy, and could not help noticing the white cap he wore. It made me dislike him hugely on sight.

7

He was tall and boyish with wide eyes, hair swept back: like Orson Welles as Harry Lime in *The Third Man*; that same moon face. He cultivated the resemblance, and I fancied I saw in the high shine of his toe-caps a vain reminder of that introduction to Lime: 'EXT. VIENNA NIGHT – Close up, black Oxfords in dark doorway.' Sometimes too he addressed me with a mocking 'Old man'.

His voice, his way of speaking, was his most arresting quality. It was a centred voice. He knew its value and exploited it. It was not accent or fluency that gave it charm, but pitch. Robinson knew by instinct what note to adopt. His was the most confidential voice I had ever heard and were he to call now I know I'd be convinced all over again. But the telephone here has stopped ringing, apart from the occasional stray call from the past, fielded by the answer machine.

The telephone was always his best medium. To me, at least, he'd just say, 'How are you?' or 'How are things?' without introducing himself, knowing I'd know. He used the phone cunningly and knew that ground could be gained where it wouldn't face to face. Sometimes during a call he'd call me Christo, which no one had done since I was a child.

Our relationship depended on half a dozen public places of Robinson's choosing. If I suggested one pub, he'd say another. If I said seven thirty, he'd say, 'Can we make it twenty minutes later?' Then he would add, as an afterthought, 'Old man, you don't mind?' Such fine tuning of the social itinerary was typical of him and I never did mind, much. Robinson liked the Wheatsheaf, north of Oxford Street, the gloomy Admiral Duncan, and the De Hems on the border of Soho's Chinatown, when it was still seedy and full of Chinese. The De Hems was closed for a while after a stabbing witnessed by Robinson. He described the victim's last moments with a clinical reverence while I imagined him, taller than the rest, leaning forward with his characteristic stare, not flinching from the gash in the throat, frothing with pink blood, or from the milky gaze of the dying man.

By then I was intrigued by Robinson, more so than when we first met on the corner of Manette Street one evening as night fell. Almost immediately we lost the person who had introduced us, a feckless and charming young man in the film business. Robinson cocked his head towards the arch at the end of the street to see if I was going his way. I nodded and we fell into step.

We passed into Greek Street under the archway that was to become our favourite entrance to the area because it was like a border-post, the crossing-point where obligations could be left behind.

We turned left. Robinson talked about how hard it was to find any remains of the shivering, naked heart of the city that Soho had once been: the countless creaking, winding stairs, leading to poky rooms, the ascendant lured up by whatever clumsy enticement was offered by the crudely hand-lettered card stuck next to the downstairs bell. On that first evening we collided with a man ducking out after his swift transaction upstairs, already moving at street speed as he came through the door.

Robinson stopped and peered at the whore's card. Written in pathetic, childish capitals was the name Monique. He looked at me. 'Do you fancy going up?'

'Not particularly.'

'Did you ever go to a whore?'

I felt a flash of irritation at this importuning, and Robinson let me see that he knew I'd been drawn. 'Oh, I'm curious, that's all,' he said lightly; eye contact, smile. His smile was frank and I decided to like him after all and to go along with whatever the evening might bring.

He started to stroll on. 'I'm all in favour of the financial transaction myself. How many fucks, do you reckon, in the history of Soho?' He speculated on the matter the length of Greek Street and into Old Compton Street. 'Ah, the statistics of sexual activity,' he said at one point. 'Was there ever a second in the history of this district when one couple or another wasn't?' Robinson continued, deep in his own burrowing. It took me a while to learn how his mind worked, in loops, and that his monologues fizzed and sparked before suddenly burning themselves out, as this one did, about halfway down Old Compton Street.

He stood staring at his shiny toe-caps. He had a small aluminium container in his hand and was shaking something from it, a pill he slipped into his mouth. This sneaky little sequence was performed with great dexterity, like a conjuring trick done to test my observation.

'It's the secrecy of it, that's the thing,' he said quietly, staring at me. 'Here, all around.' He addressed me as though I were backward, and gestured with his head up at the lighted windows above. 'Go to the suburbs and take a look at the houses at night and you know nothing's going on. Am I right?'

He made the question sound both rhetorical and uncomfortably personal. One of the windows went dark and a few doors down another lit up. Smart young couples drifted past, up from the suburbs for a night out. Robinson caught my hesitation.

'A married man, I'll bet,' he said.

I shrugged.

'Ah, fuck your wife!' he said and walked off.

I watched his departing back, the sway of his elegant overcoat. The click of his shoes: metal quarters on the heels, I decided. The ambiguity of the insult was clever, and now I know him better, calculated. At the time I thought I could take or leave such smart talk.

I felt unsettled by Robinson's insult, long after the event. For reasons I was at a loss to understand, I found myself wanting to explain to him, but what I was not sure. He drifted through my peripheral vision, a shadowy, nagging figure. Several sightings added to the unease. One lunchtime, when I was buying sandwiches, he walked by outside, and in pubs I noticed him with a raffish crowd and avoided his gaze.

We met again on an unusually crowded evening in the George in Wardour Street, running into each other at the bar while waiting to be served. 'Here, let me,' he said. 'What are you having?' I told him I was already buying a round. He looked at the swaggering film crowd I was drinking with and asked if I was one of them. I shrugged. He seemed amused at this. 'You don't look the type.'

Robinson insisted on paying for the drinks and I wondered why, perhaps he wanted an introduction. We stood in silence watching the barmaid serve us. He seemed to be on his own. When his scotch came he downed it while my beers were still being drawn. 'Cheers,' he said, smartly putting the empty glass back on the bar. He paid for the round and raised an eyebrow. 'Perhaps run into you again.' Then he was gone, with no apology offered for his previous behaviour. I was surprised not to feel more irritated. Instead I felt curious, at the extent to which our paths were crossing, and flattered, in spite of my better judgement, as though he were seeking me out.

When Robinson wasn't in the George, he was usually to be found in the Blue Posts soon after five thirty, sitting upstairs in a lounge bar left over from the Fifties, in front of him the gin that he took to set himself up for the evening. He liked to observe the ebb and flow of the couple of hours after opening. First, the hurried drinks taken straight after work by office types, who downed their glasses in quick succession, blew their resolutions to be home by seven and left loudly and uncertainly between forty to fifty minutes late. Then came the arrival of those who had gone home, changed and come back to make a night of it. Robinson could calculate the exact time of the hiatus, usually no more than twenty minutes, between the two squashes.

Those early drinks must have been at the end of the winter because he still wore the long dark coat he'd had on when we'd first met. 'Fancy another?' Robinson would ask, cocking his empty glass. Where's the harm in that, I would wonder.

Once settled in the pub it became hard to leave. Decisions and anxieties receded, and on a good night it was possible to make that comfortable state of semi-intoxication last two or three hours before drunkennesses set in. Often we stayed to closing time and then went on somewhere else where we could get a last drink. I enjoyed these binges and they became more frequent as the weeks went by. It must have occurred to me that I knew next to nothing about Robinson, but that seemed not to be the point. He was a constant fact at a time when everyone else was uncertain: the reliable drinking companion.

Soon it was warm enough to stand and drink in the street and watch the first bare limbs of the year. Robinson without his overcoat kept his impression of darkness, not of fashionable black but of something more permanent. Daylight seemed to make him restless; only with dusk did he relax. He never seemed in any hurry to end the evening.

When I missed the last tube, I sometimes had a hard time finding a taxi prepared to drive out so far. I was often short of cash and would have to search the house for spare change while the knocking diesel engine of the waiting cab started to wake the street. A few times I borrowed off Robinson, who always carried a fat wad in his back pocket held in a money clip. The clip had a ruby embedded in it, unusually flashy for him.

One night, I wound up in Oxford Street, drunk and with no money. I returned to where Robinson had been but he had moved on. The air in the street was electric and clammy. When the storm broke the only warning was a few large, dark splashes hitting the pavement: the roar that followed drowned the noise of the city in seconds. Cars passed in silence as I ran, drenched, to the office to wait for the storm to pass. There I fell asleep without meaning to.

The office belonged to a small film company run by the improbably named Johnny Repp. I remember Robinson asking early in our drinking days if it were his real name. Originally Greek, I thought, the dopolous part of it lost quite recently. 'Johnny the Greek,' said Robinson with a laugh. 'Sounds like you can't stand him.' Few could.

Repp employed a handful of wideboys who liked to be thought of as wolves: hand carelessly over the telephone mouthpiece – caller hanging on – instructions shouted through the open door to the secretary to tell the next caller to fuck off, then sweetly into the receiver, 'Not you, John.' Feet were swung on to the desk, the phone cradled lovingly into the neck and a grin fixed in place (they grinned on the phone, always). Their distinguishing features in business were a mixture of jargon, flirtation – 'If we're going to get into bed together' was a fashionable office cliché that summer – and cheerful aggression: 'Do us a favour, go on, fuck off.' They necked casually in the office with the company molls (all carefully vetted by Repp), and, if anyone came into the room, said things like, 'Excuse me if I don't stand up, I've got a hard-on.' Robinson called them the condomin-the-wallet boys.

After work they went round in a pack, drinking in pubs, and furiously arguing over business they were too disorganised to fit into the day, though they always appeared busy, unlike myself. They infuriated me: their passionate squabbling, their nursery mentality, their effortless spiel and self-aggrandisement, their involvement, the bits of power-play, quite byzantine in their sloppy elaborateness. I was jealous. My own career was becalmed and my nerve not holding, which was why I had exchanged freelancing for a dubious executive status.

I re-read Fitzgerald's *The Crack-Up* travelling in and out on the Underground. I told myself, not without satisfaction, that I'd burned out before my time. There was even a sense of achievement in this, a compensation for a larger failure. (I had nothing much to my name – a handful of scripts, more often filmed than not, none as good as I'd once thought.) I was drawn to emulate Fitzgerald's crash, though realising (not enough of the time) I'd done nothing to earn it. Either way, I found myself not putting up with things in the way I once did.

I discovered I liked the quiet and white of the office when no one was there. Later on, during the mild nights of midsummer, I would sleep there, on a piece of flat roof, in a sleeping-bag bought for the purpose. The office was down a quiet mews through a low archway, under which derelicts drank cider and sweet sherry, a former sweat shop and probably stables before that. My own room had only a skylight, and the absence of windows lent a mood of detention to each day. The rest of the place was a warren of stairs, rooms within rooms and crooked corridors that I took to exploring when I had the place to myself. A disused flight of stairs led up to a set of attic rooms. They were empty and covered with dust, neglected for years, apparently, except by pigeons and mice, the walls faded from, at a guess, cream to something the colour of the North Sea on a rough day. An old toilet still worked and there was a basin that ran cold water. Bare wooden floors were still littered with buttons dropped by seamstresses. They crunched underfoot and sparkled in moonlight. When the weather was bad I dragged the sleeping bag inside and listened to the rain and the occasional shout or smash of an empty bottle from the derelicts under the arch. I told no one about the attic except my wife. If she thought my behaviour strange, she made no comment.

There was an old song on a juke box in one of the pubs where Robinson and I drank that went, *It was fun for a while*, which was how I felt about my double life. I became accomplished at hiding in the attic, with a change or two of clothes and a little primus stove for coffee, all carefully stowed away to prevent discovery.

I took lunch alone in a cavernous basement through which Chinese waitresses pushed trolleys of dim-sum in round wooden boxes, and afterwards browsed in the stackrooms of bookshops in the Charing Cross Road. I was spending more and more time underground and wondered at that. In rare moments of clarity, I realised I was cutting myself adrift and wondered at that too.

The daily afternoon meeting, or conference, as Repp preferred to call it, was held under his disconcerting, unblinking gaze, behind spectacle lenses that grew darker as the sun moved round and made everything in the room bright and pale beside the black pools of his eyes. These sessions were invariably interrupted by a transatlantic call from Repp's partner, Dennis. No one was sure if it was his first or last name because he had always been known only as Dennis. He was a modern-day Cortez on speed, an explorer of that strange abstract territory of figures and estimates, his voyages epic searches through hostile office space after finance for low-budget films. His time was spent flying in and out of Los Angeles where he ran up a fortune in limousine bills because he couldn't drive.

Repp's paranoia reduced him to running the company from his room, hence the constant meetings. These gatherings served little purpose beyond letting him behave as though he were still the wisecracking bully at the back of class, his favourite weapon the sneaky aside delivered within hearing. The particular butt of his cruel streak was Truefitt, the odd one out in the office, clumsy, keen and forever miscalculating, like the time he arrived at a meeting wearing shorts and was singled out, once more, as the victim of Repp's merciless double-take. I felt something of Repp's contempt at the sight of Truefitt tugging miserably at his shorts for the rest of the meeting, and this later disturbed me. Until then I'd not taken Repp's bullying seriously and had even gone along with it because Truefitt's own dogged earnestness seemed enough of a defence, a form of condoning. It made me wonder if Repp weren't responsible for my own frustration in a way that I had failed to identify.

These dog days in the office coincided with my initiation into Robinson's social circle. If the afternoons were slow I put that down to anticipating what the evenings might bring. Robinson was going through a gregarious phase and had access to an attractive crowd, elegant, easy-going, well off and attended by apparently available women whose creamy limbs were surely inaccessible. Plucked eyebrows were arched in expressions of permanent, blank surprise, and their perfect white teeth made me sparing with my own smile. They looked like cover girls, dressed like models, and seemed to find life effortless.

I learned early on to take the simple precaution of

having a couple of stiff gins before arriving. Then the nights became seamless, fuelled by alcohol and, occasionally, by one of Robinson's little pills, which made me feel bright and focused. Time ran smooth and everything became reckless and provocative. Meals passed gazing in admiration at this nocturnal breed, or in surreptitious study of a neck or a wrist, while I drank exotic cocktails and fantasised about these superior creatures.

Usually Robinson reserved the same large table in a fashionable restaurant where a dozen or more of us sat down to dinner. He went out of his way to be charming and intriguing (answering a question with a question), his deliberate reticence about himself calculated to provoke speculation. Everyone had a different angle on Robinson, who was at his most Gatsby-like during this period, mixing high and low life at the same table, seating rebellious young aristocrats next to a former criminal associate of the Krays who explained how to saw off the barrel of a shotgun. 'Dangerous thing to do, now looking back on it,' he told me. 'But they were available, yeah, and they were usable.' He fixed me with a dead stare perfected in the course of thousands of protection money collections.

A striking looking woman with blonde hair, which she wore pinned up, sat on my left. Her name was Sonia and we exchanged the usual banalities, in between conversation with the heavy about making a film about the old East End rackets. 'I don't like the word gangster,' he warned me. 'It's not like that, it embarrasses me.' Robinson looked up, caught my eye and raised his glass with a dry smile.

Sonia asked what I knew about Robinson. 'Not much,' I replied. It was generally acknowledged that he was some kind of dealer, though in what no one was sure. Her version included rumours of inherited wealth (I'd heard that too) and large storage containers somewhere in South London. She leaned forward confidingly, revealing a smudge of cleavage. 'Nobody knows what he keeps in them.'

She asked if I found Robinson ambiguous. I shrugged lightly and returned the question. 'As a woman, no,' she said. 'But I can see how men might.' We laughed, having reached that stage of the evening when everything seemed amusing.

She let me kiss her in the back of a taxi we shared. Fresh lipstick smeared invitingly. Outside her flat we kissed again – watched in the rear-view mirror by the taxi driver – less successfully. The easy conversation of the restaurant seemed an age ago as we exchanged stilted goodbyes. She smiled vaguely and offered her cheek. The driver shrugged.

At home my erratic hours were explained by pressure of work and necessary socialising. I blamed my infrequent appearances on Repp's chaotic impulses, a strategy that required little fabrication. Besides, Repp's partner Dennis was always flying in and out. Sometimes I pretended to go with him.

Without my noticing, an invisible line was crossed, one that distinguishes a project that is merely in development from those that are suddenly bound to get made. Though it was far from the case that ours was certain, Repp started to behave as though there were green lights all the way, and the days became hectic. Provisional schedules were drawn up, directors put on shortlists, technicians interviewed. Repp's time was spent in continual discussion with financiers, accountants, film studios, lighting companies, drumming up interest, no matter that once the project became official these people would beat a path to his door of their own accord. 'Everyone wants to do business with us,' he told me with the phony sincerity that was his trademark. The fact of the matter was that he was telling everyone the film had a start date when he had neither a complete script nor all his financing, let alone a director.

There were increasingly long discussions with various special effects and prosthetic experts about whether a diabolical little creature that resembled an ordinary doll in the script was going to be a remote-controlled dummy or a midget in some sort of costume. Artists were hired to make drawings, and still no one could decide.

Robinson quizzed me incessantly about these dreary, humourless meetings, which he then related to others, making them sound like hours of knockabout fun, mimicking the droning zeal of these earnest young experts on the difficulty of creating accurate reproductions of close-range gunshot wounds to the head. Fascinated by these ingenious bores, he asked me to bring one to the pub, but when I did he lasted ten minutes before downing his drink and making his excuses.

Sonia continued to let herself be kissed in the back of taxis and left it at that. When she wasn't at the restaurant I tried to catch the last tube home, and started to sleep past my stop, ending up on drunken looping walks through obscure suburban streets in search of a night bus or a 24-hour minicab. Either way, I was spending a fortune on fares.

The mornings in the attic when I failed to wake up before the others arrived for work became more frequent. Then I would be woken by a telephone ringing in the office downstairs or the clack-clack of the photocopy machine directly below. Some days I pretended I was out at meetings and began to fabricate schedules in advance. My work diary became a log-book of appointments that would never take place.

One night, after dropping Sonia, I returned on impulse to Soho. Robinson was amused by my reappearance. 'Well, fancy.' He was sitting in a club where he liked to end his evening, by himself and as self-contained as ever. He seemed in a genial mood and said he had something to show me.

He took me round the corner to a multi-storey car park. 'Where are we going?' I asked in the lift. We got off at the top floor.

'Fancy a drive?' he asked, throwing me a set of keys. I fumbled and dropped them.

'Is this yours?' I asked, surprised at the shiny black Jaguar. Robinson shrugged nonchalantly. 'Go on, give it a go. I trust you.' I unlocked the car and he climbed in the back and stretched out. I was well over the limit and drunk enough not to care.

The car seemed to drive itself, responding to the merest suggestion, whispering forward with us cocooned in leather-bound silence, protected behind the Cinemascope windscreen. We cruised past Warren Street, jumped red lights on the Euston Road and hit eighty on the Westway with Robinson hooting with laughter and shouting, 'Faster, faster,' as the speedometer crept towards a hundred. Afterwards I thanked him. I hadn't enjoyed myself so much in a long time.

The next time Robinson and I went cruising he asked Sonia too. To my annoyance she sat with Robinson. He put a tape into a machine built especially into the back of the car and something operatic smoothed our way forward. We glided through the night streets and under his instructions drove east through a district of tower blocks. I had pleasant double-vision and the most deli-cate finger-tip control. I was strangely exhilarated by these drunken night drives. By day I was dimly aware of this being a sign that all was not well, that the various compartments of my life were not in quite the order I pretended. But, for the moment, I was happy to be guided by Robinson who divined my repressed sense of recklessness.

'You drive very well,' said Robinson. He was smirking. 'You should come and work for me.' He turned to Sonia. 'He could be my driver, what do you think? Should we make him put on the uniform?' I fancied he had his hand on her knee.

We looped back round through the river and out towards Woolwich and Charlton where Robinson made me turn off the main road down sidestreets of dingy terrace housing. As we wound our way through the maze of streets, it became clear that our apparently aimless journey had a destination. Robinson guided us until we were in a particular road and outside a house where he made me stop. Gentrification had not reached this far out and the street was run down, the house shabbier than most. A light burned dully in the ground floor bay window.

Robinson got out of the car without explanation and knocked on the door, though it was past one in the morning. I wondered if we were visiting a scene from his childhood and being afforded a privileged glimpse into his past. Sonia had the same thought. 'Do you think it's his mother?' she asked. Neither of us was expecting the tall, poised black woman who answered the door. She looked misplaced and too well dressed for such surroundings.

Robinson stood on the step declining her invitation to go inside. He stayed a few minutes only, chatting and laughing, more relaxed than I'd seen him. The woman smiled, and stood with her arms folded, one foot stretched forward so that only the spike of her heel rested on the ground. She looked like a dancer. When he left he handed her an envelope. They kissed, her hand resting lightly on the back of his neck. In spite of their intimacy it was impossible to say whether they were or had been lovers.

The drive back was tense and disjointed. I felt tired and drunk. We had been passing a bottle of brandy around between us. The scene we had just witnessed had irritated me, perhaps because of its obvious tenderness and the sudden exclusion of Sonia and myself. The mood of these drives was essentially one of complicity, or so I had thought. Robinson lost his temper when I insisted on knowing who the woman was and I got annoyed at his reticence, and told him so, until he said, 'She was someone who looked after me when I was young.' I didn't believe him. 'I couldn't give a fuck what you believe,' he said tartly.

'Drive your own fucking car,' was all I could think to say. Robinson gave me a sour look in the mirror and I fancied Sonia's hand was inside his fly.

I didn't see the running man until it was too late. Sonia squealed at me to watch out. And in the rear-view mirror I saw Robinson alert and expectant as the man filled the windscreen, his face white in the car lights. He hung for a second like a cutout target in the sights of the Jaguar, the dark empty street spread out like a poster behind. I accelerated at him, then braked and brought the car under control thirty or forty yards later. Robinson got out and went back.

Sonia hugged the front seat. The atmosphere was charged. She was lucky, she could have gone through the windscreen. I imagined kissing her, thinking of her cry and how erotic it had sounded. I wondered about driving off without Robinson. Sonia sat back and lit a cigarette with a steady hand.

I went and joined Robinson. He was standing over the man, who was sitting on the kerb, rubbing his shin where I had clipped him with the bumper of the Jaguar. The man seemed all right, just shaken. He was a rummy, and not in any state to work out what had happened, so we left him sucking on the last of our brandy. I told

Robinson he should drive but he ignored me and climbed in the back. He and Sonia sat apart, I was glad to see.

On the drive back he demonstrated to her the principles of hitting and missing a moving target, explaining how by driving straight at the man I had avoided him. Had I swerved the way he was running we would have collided and probably killed him. He whacked the palm of his hand with his fist, making a sickening thud. 'Smart work, old man,' he said in a deadpan voice.

Robinson knew I'd intended running the man down. I also knew he had wanted me to, was willing me, and was disappointed I had missed. I felt like someone who had flunked a test and at the same time was appalled at what I was getting myself into.

We dropped Sonia off. Finally I said to him, 'I'm not up for these weird games.'

'What weird games?'

I shut up, having neither the patience nor the inclination for any more of Robinson's interrogatory tricks. After a while he said, 'Just along for the ride, are we?' I ignored him.

At the next set of lights he got out abruptly and told me to take the Jaguar back to the garage. 'Leave the keys at the kiosk.' I did without being sure why; serve him right if I abandoned it with the keys in the ignition.

Back in the attic, and nursing more brandy, I felt a mean and fragile high. Controlled recklessness, that was the thing.

The film suddenly stopped being made, only a couple of weeks before shooting was due to begin, when one part of the finance inexplicably fell through. Recrimination was in the air: blame the script, whose fault, fire accordingly. New writers would be found, further scapegoats

23

hired. I was tired of the false deadlines, the artificial pan-ics, so many speculative meetings, too much lying. The script wouldn't be ready on the first day of shooting – if there ever were such a thing – because now the film was having to be done on the cheap and the budget had been shaved. There would be cuts and revisions right up until the end of filming. The whole thing was as rickety as a house of cards.

My days became footloose. If Repp noticed my erratic hours he said nothing. Access to him was increasingly cut off. There were times when I wanted nothing more than to ask for a meeting and have it out, but he fobbed me off. I knew my days were numbered.

The restaurant nights continued, without Sonia who disappeared off the scene. Robinson gave no explanation for her absence. Towards me, he went out of his way to appear solicitous. Once he looked at me and asked, 'Are you all right, old man?' I was able to shrug off the question. I had a summer cold, caught off Robinson, and was able to blame that.

I carried on spending time in Soho and continued to stay some nights in the attic, not telling anyone what I was doing, sometimes meeting people for lunch, as though everything were normal. The mornings started at the Bar Italia: *espressi* taken standing at the zinc counter, while in the background on a huge video screen Italy versus Brazil and the Rossi goals that took the *azzuri* to the World Cup final were replayed for the millionth time. I tried to remember to have a spot to eat. Book-shops were good for passing time, then a couple of drinks while reading the paper cover to cover and the luxury of being able to sit in an empty pub so soon after morning opening. For lunch I met acquaintances with expense accounts (avoiding those in the film business) and managed not to pay. I made it the main meal of the day – got to keep the stomach lined on these jags –

drinking white wine, saving red for the evening.

There was plenty to occupy me during the slow hung-over mornings. My drinking was becoming indiscriminate, and attempts to retrace the voyage of the night before invariably faltered because gaps were starting to appear – great white spaces like unexplored territory on a map. At first the discovery of these spaces was disconcerting, but I learned to see in them a not unpleasant sense of mystery. With practice I learned to make the extra effort to note, in the course of an evening's degeneration, a handful of signs for later: a look, a phrase, the arrival of a fresh drink or remark made to a waiter. All could act as possible markers, as though establishing a criminal alibi.

My horizons shrank until I found it hard to leave the area. It felt as though I would be breaking a spell. Even when lunch was spun out until three and later it was tiring wandering around waiting for evening, so I started napping for an hour or two in one of the cinemas. Soho cinemas showed nothing but porno films. There was no other sort in the area, apart from the film trade preview theatres – dark little rooms around Wardour Street – that belonged to a fraternity I wanted to avoid.

The porno cinemas were well behind what Robinson called the skirting board of society. To stand in the gloom of the entrance to the auditorium, eyes adjusting to the dark, was to become aware of a slowly developing picture of magnificent furtiveness: upturned faces, pale and as hushed and expectant as communicants at an altar rail. And the cinema was always full, not half-empty as you might expect: so many of us down there was my first impression; middle-aged men, white and white collar, and a lot of younger Asians. The films were foreign and full of badly dubbed grunts. The actors went through the motions with an air of detachment, and the women, in the act of spreading themselves, appeared to retreat beyond reach into private reverie. A lot of noise was what the punters liked, to cover their own rustlings. Sometimes the whole audience swayed as though bucketed by a tempest, and the seats creaked louder than the soundtrack.

These trips to the porno cinemas, which started out as an excuse for a rest, became an end in themselves, pleasantly secretive at first – furtive enjoyment, why not? – then compulsive: blurred afternoons that didn't do anyone harm is what I told myself.

The voyeur I noticed only because he was in my line of vision when I woke up. He sat twisted around in the front row, watching the audience watching the film. His spectacles caught the light from the projector, at least so I thought until I saw they were binoculars, used to study faces in the audience, my own at that particular moment.

I saw him several times, always in the front row. He made a point of singling me out. It turned out he wore glasses as well. Once I passed near enough to make out Coke-bottle lenses and a mirthless grin. I half-expected to run across him in the street, where I would have known him at once, though I'd not seen him in anything other than the semi-gloom of the auditorium; the house lights in porno cinemas stayed dimmed even during intervals. Once I thought I caught a glimpse of him in Archer Street, with Robinson, but decided it must have been a dream. I never mentioned the porno cinemas to Robinson.

Most of my energy went into organising my Jekyll and Hyde life, an exhausting concoction of evasions, excuses and alibis. I told my wife I was away on business for a fortnight in California. We talked wistfully about meeting up somewhere, to try to mend what was broken, though both of us knew it was beyond repair.

My relationship with Robinson moved by tacit agreement into darker waters. When we found ourselves at a loose end after an evening, we idly started to follow people for a few blocks to see where they went, betting on which way they would go. Then we began shadowing drunks. The drunker they were the more Robinson appeared to enjoy himself. Staggering couples weaved their uncertain way, cannoning off each other and back, then falling into dark doorways where they clung together, fumbling, helpless, suddenly fidgety with lust. At this point, Robinson would leave them to it, rather to my surprise. Usually I was drunk enough to want to stay only where I was. The next day, when sober, I felt bad about our nocturnal wanderings, tailing those more helpless than myself, though in the drunken slipstream of Robinson I secretly enjoyed these vignettes of incapacity, and the guilty pleasure and vicarious power I felt from watching them. I wondered too if they were not part of some strategy on Robinson's part. The logic I used to justify these excursions involved my having to be with him because his capacity for enormous violence was held in check only by my restraining presence. I'd not seen this violence yet, but knew it was there. Once, in one of the alleys connecting Wardour and Dean, we came across a man passed out in a doorway, a man in a suit, not a derelict. Robinson bet me that I didn't have the nerve to roll him. 'You'd like to, but you daren't.'

Sometimes Robinson approached the drunks. He'd ask for a cigarette and scrounge one, and produce a light for both of them, hands cupped carefully around the flame of an old Dunhill lighter he carried, though he did not smoke. (The cigarettes were passed on to me.) Not until he had produced the Dunhill a number of times did it strike me how little Robinson carried in the way of personal possessions. The money clip, the aluminium container of pills and the lighter were all I'd seen. I assumed the lighter was of sentimental value, but Robinson said he had found it. I doubted this since there was so much he chose not to carry: no watch, no address book, no scraps of paper, no cheque books, no credit cards, none of the junk or bits of identification that most people accumulate.

One evening Robinson sifted idly through my own wallet and found more than a dozen samples of my signature on bank and credit cards and their receipts, two passport size photographs of myself, a driving licence that I had forgotten to sign, two other records of my address and various scraps of paper with telephone numbers scribbled on them. Robinson asked who the numbers belonged to and I couldn't be sure.

When my wrist watch stopped I did not bother to wind it again, a little act of self-consciousness that I saw as a symbol of my present condition. I would let everything run down, then start over again. Any misgivings I had – and there were plenty swarming just below the surface – I suppressed or forgot in alcohol. In drink I discovered a fluency that never found its way into words.

I woke up in a porno cinema, with no memory of getting there, in urgent need of a piss. I shoved my way down the row, past grumbling punters as a scene reached its noisy climax on the screen. The walk to the toilet made me realise how drunk I was, not quite incapable but walking an awkward path too close to an unseen drop. Two exit signs over the door, shut one eye and they slid into one – in the land of the blind – a final falsetto scream from the soundtrack and the audience shuddered to its climax, and the whole cinema fell quiet, apart from the late-comers. I laughed to myself as I barged through the toilet door. Someone was already stood at the first of the two urinals, and I had to push past. I took care not to be careless, because of the drink, and piss on my shoes. The toilets were the bowl sort fixed to the wall, which made it easier.

The other man was just standing there, doing nothing by the sound of it. I splashed about with a worldly air, stuffed my free hand into my pocket and told myself I didn't know a man that didn't sneak a look at the fellow standing next to him in a public toilet. I glanced out of the corner of my eye. The sight made no sense, even taking into account looking askance and double vision: two of them standing at the same urinal. I looked harder: two, definitely; one tiny though, it seemed, and held up by the other so his feet rested on the rim of the bowl. A child in a porno cinema toilet? I aimed at the cubes of disinfectant in the urinal (a dainty touch considering the nature of the establishment). Surreptitious movements to my right: not hard to guess what they were up to. The sugar cubes were pitted where I'd pissed on them, and when the urinal flushed itself automatically they floated. I stood there, drunk, fly undone, waiting to see if I became aroused. I wondered if I'd become infected by Robinson, if he had passed on to me a clinical inquisitiveness, akin to a virus, that made the contemplation of anything permissible. The shock was not in the scene, but in my own suddenly alert curiosity.

Then the child – Christ, what was I doing standing there? – turned his head, and I looked up expecting to see an angel boy with the eyes of a sewer rat. Instead, staring at me were the thick, round little lenses of the voyeur. The transformation was more than I could grasp. How had he got there? Perhaps I had blanked out. Then I saw. The voyeur was a dwarf being held up by another man to a urinal that he couldn't otherwise reach. (In a lurch of puddled logic I remembered dreary meetings with Repp about how to make a diabolical mechanical doll convincing in our movie, and here was the answer, except none of it mattered any more.) I stumbled back to the auditorium and woke up much later with a miserable hangover.

Robinson was in a vile mood that evening. I had sobered up, drinking tomato juices when it was my round, pretending they were bloody marys, and was spoiling for a fight. Then I drank too much in the half hour before closing and was drunk again. I'd tried to draw Robinson out, to get him to answer questions about himself, like where his money came from – another fat roll I saw that night – and why he never carried anything of note, but he was having none of it and went off to talk to someone else down the other end of the bar. I sat there helpless, incapable of decisions, protected by the dull noise of the pub. It was the De Hems we were in, where Robinson had witnessed the stabbing. It was nicely done out now, the Chinese clientele gone, more like a singles bar. I looked carefully at the women.

'Do you fancy her?' Robinson asked when he found me staring at a tall woman who looked bored and drunk. The man with her was the worse for wear, and by then everyone else in the pub was too. Robinson seemed cheered up. I'd forgotten what our quarrel was about and was quite happy to go along with whatever he suggested.

We ended up following the drunk couple. The cool night air made them even more lightheaded and helpless as they tottered up Greek Street. I missed my footing once or twice but was still capable of imitating someone more sober than myself. Robinson was silent and had about him the air of a stalker.

Twenty or thirty yards ahead of us, the couple turned right into Manette Street (where Robinson and I had first met). We went through the arch to find the man retching copiously over some railings, and the woman flat on the pavement, skirt ridden up over her knees, one shoe dangling, eyes fluttering. I watched the man as he dry heaved, prelude to a second bout of vomiting. As his buttocks clenched with each spasm, the wallet in his hip pocket nudged into view, there for the taking, as was the woman. Robinson was assuming command. I urgently wanted to crack the vomiting man's teeth with my shoe, to catch him full force as he bowed to retch, snapping his head back so the puke shot out his mouth in a backward arc. Jesus, aren't I the fucking dandy? Robinson was helping the woman to her feet, and ordered me to find a cab. Ah fuck you too, I thought, and slouched off to the end of the street, but there weren't any in the Charing Cross Road just then. One with its light on didn't stop. When I got back Robinson and the woman had done a bunk. Where the fuck were they? The man was still clinging to the railings. His wallet was on the pavement. I picked it up. The man took off his glasses and got that sleepy, vulnerable look some people get without their spectacles. I asked where Robinson and the woman were but he couldn't make sense of the question. He managed to fold his glasses all right, but it took a long time, and when he tried to put them away he kept missing and snagging the top of his pocket. He snorted and looked helpless. I told him to gaze up at the stars, it would make him feel better and, when he did, he lost his footing and sat down on his arse with a bump and looked so surprised I didn't have the gall to kick him in the mouth as I'd promised myself. I still felt like stamping on his spectacles, which had fallen on the ground. Instead I picked them up and stuffed them in his top pocket.

I was going to send back the wallet the next day and had got as far as the post office when I remembered what I had in mind and hung on to it.

When I next saw Robinson he was with the couple from Manette Street. I felt a bit queasy as I spotted them and was about to slip off when he saw me and made introductions. The man blinked behind his glasses and showed no sign of recognition. We shook hands while Robinson looked smug, as though he were bringing us together for some purpose. I wondered if the whole thing had been a set-up and half-expected Robinson to remove the wallet deftly from my pocket and return it to the man as though completing some conjuring trick. He'd had the woman, of that I had no doubt.

The man with glasses and the woman were not a couple, as I'd thought, so he didn't care half as much as I did that she had gone off with Robinson. I suspected that their version of what had happened – that the man had said he'd find his own way when he felt well enough – was not accurate. I was sure they had dumped him. Robinson and the woman went around together for a while.

I liked the way I contrived to pass the wallet on to Robinson. After transferring its contents to my own wallet, I casually dropped it in the Blue Posts thinking he was bound to notice. Instead he ignored it and eventually I asked if it were his. He replied that he didn't have one (as I suspected). I pressed him to take it. The gesture was meant as a back-handed joke since Robinson never carried anything to put in a wallet. It felt right, the idea of him carrying an empty wallet.

Occasionally, I inspected the new contents of my wallet: the credit cards (whose signature I practised with no success) and receipts with phone numbers scribbled on, belonging to the man with glasses. I phoned these numbers to see who would answer and, depending on the voice at the end of the line, I either hung up or said I was a friend of the man with glasses and had they seen him or did they have his number because I had lost it? One woman sounded friendly. I called her a few times – with various excuses – before she got suspicious and I spoilt things by hanging up in a hurry.

I started seeing the woman from Manette Street who

had been going around with Robinson. 'Take her, old man. She's all yours,' he had said. He was always generous with things that weren't his to give. I took her nevertheless, but as Robinson had been there first my efforts were half-hearted. She was still in touch with him and probably reported on my lack of prowess. I suspected Robinson fed off self-destructiveness in others, that his talent was for spotting weaknesses and he enjoyed exploiting them. I was sure he could be malicious.

I also sensed he was growing bored with me and moving on. His absences became more frequent and prolonged. In a fit of drunken boredom, I borrowed his car one night after he had stood me up. The keys were in the multi-storey kiosk, the Jaguar waiting in its usual place on the roof. To hell with it, I thought as I drove off, Robinson owes me.

I drove out of the centre, beyond the meter zones, and parked in a back street, by some railway arches where I fell asleep and dreamed of the wreckage of too many late nights. I was one of those wired-up dummies in test car crashes: the gathering speed, cruising way over the limit, faster and faster, until, no warning, BLOW OUT: too late to stop, crash coming, spasm on impact. ('*Spasm on impact*', I can hear Robinson saying, 'would be a great title for a film.' It would not.) Then I saw myself in a lift where the light was too bright, with a woman I did not know; my sullen reflection, caught unawares in a mirror, was unrecognisable in its slack vacancy. An inverted narcissism was the operating principle of these nights. Crash of bodies, accidental scrape of teeth, heavy limbs rearranged into a mutual geometry of calculated desire; an open country road – grainy like a home movie – driven at speed, empty and fast and straight, crossroads way in the distance, suddenly much closer, vehicle intersection, too late now.

I stayed in the Jaguar, slept off my binge and thought

about Robinson and tried to make sense of my theory that he didn't actually exist. He was both as substantial and as thin as a character in a movie. Robinson was there, all right, a character, but all the little things about him – the lack of identification, the use of cash – suggested someone outside everything. His ability to operate in the present threw me, made me try to obliterate my own past with excursions into white space. I had dismantled my life so thoroughly until all that remained was a discard pile of cut-up gestures, like an unedited film sequence, bits missing. I was left in the position of playing voyeur to myself.

I returned the Jaguar, went back to the suburbs, broke with the old places, and made an effort to change, though this did not happen all at once. I saw Robinson once more several weeks later, after I'd forgotten my paranoia and thought I had shaken off his influence. We ran into each other in an after-hours bar where to get in it was necessary only to sign the members' book with enough of a flourish. He was sitting at the bar, with Sonia. She was friendlier than expected. Robinson raised an eyebrow and smiled. I was with other people, so we exchanged little more than a brief hello. We were both drunk, but he was well inside his limit and I was at the top of the slide. In his usual secretive way he suggested he was caught up in important work. I thought of the money roll in his back pocket.

His final gesture was to offer me back the wallet I had taken from the man with glasses. The Harry Lime smile, the raised eyebrow, again. 'Old man? More use to you than me, I would have thought.' I told him to keep it. How much he knew I never knew.

I took to drinking alone in suburban pubs, always within the final boundaries of the city, driving at random until, exhausted and on the cusp of a hangover, I was in some strange place, a cul-de-sac in a modern estate, perhaps.

In the pearl of early morning, I drove soberly and carefully back, merging with the first commuters, perhaps even passing for one. Moon on the wane, high over the city, pale crescent in the lightening sky; on an elevated expressway a quick burst of speed, all undone by the slow choke of the Euston Road.

I quit drinking altogether, still stayed away from the centre, and took to driving by night to Heathrow, warm nights with the window down and the radio on, out to Terminal Three. I treated the waiting lounges as my own. The nocturnal transit passengers sprawled on benches, all of them my friends, among whom I patrolled, a gracious host at the end of a party. Other times I waited in vain anticipation of a chance meeting with someone known – 'Where are you going?' – or with some stranger, selected by what process I never could decide. I was amiable, relaxed, fraudulent, my mind telescopic, cross-haired, seeking the pulse of blood, imagining its blossom. I saw myself in a crowd, taller than the rest, leaning forward with an unblinking gaze of curiosity, searching for Robinson.

Dry days followed, full of oppressive heat. I stayed indoors with the blinds down, reading and sleeping while the house was empty, going out at night. I patched things up with my wife as best I could. She had her own life which was why she put up with me. The reason I gave for being at home was that Repp had commissioned me to write a screenplay.

If it wasn't too hot I sat in the garden, getting a tan. When the weather broke I watched daytime TV. They were not unpleasant, those late summer months.

Nobody called. Sometimes I tested Robinson's number for an answer, ringing off as soon as his machine came on.

Then one day, early in autumn, he answered. I was too surprised to speak. He guessed. We agreed to meet at a reception he had been invited to. 'I'm not drinking now,' I warned. He laughed and said, 'So much the better.'

The party took place behind a huge plate-glass window in a gallery off Bond Street. It was a film crowd, I noted, with a sinking heart. I waited across the street, trying to spot Robinson.

After fifteen minutes there was no sign of him. I was about to leave when someone took my elbow from behind and I turned, expecting to be met by Robinson's ironic eyebrow. But it was Truefitt, definitely smarter and more in control. His hair was sleeked back like a Buenos Aires banker.

'I thought it was you. How are you?'

'Fine,' I answered. 'Never better.'

'He still thinks you're ill, you know.'

'Who does?'

'Repp, of course.'

Truefitt did look altogether different. New horn-rim glasses gave him a serious air. For some reason he had covered for me with Repp, telling him I was away sick with glandular fever.

'Come in, it's not that bad, really.' Seeing my hesitation, he added that Repp wasn't expected. 'Shooting starts in three days and the financing still isn't a hundred per cent.' 'Is the script ready?' I asked. Truefitt laughed and offered me a cigarette. 'You know, I watched him grind you down.' It was my turn to laugh. 'And all the time I thought you were the one he was grinding down,' I said. Truefitt smiled ruefully, lit our cigarettes and blew a confident plume of smoke from the corner of his mouth. I was annoyed with Robinson.

The gallery was crowded and hot; loosened ties and

little beads of perspiration on make-up. I sipped orange juice, and felt awkward enough to want to leave until I got cornered by some woman drunk enough to mistake me for someone else.

She wore a pillbox hat with a veil. I asked her where she had got it. She told me and added, 'Not that you care.' She had on a heart-shaped dress that showed a promising amount of bosom. She didn't know anyone and had an interesting drawl.

The shrieks of laughter that greeted whatever I said, funny or not, indicated more than plain drunkenness, more like imminent loss of control. I saw she was very young. She laid a confiding hand on my arm and asked me to hold her drink because she had drunk too much as it was. I checked the room for Robinson and when I next looked at her she had another full glass in her hand and I was still holding hers. 'God, I'm so pissed,' she repeated. 'What's to eat?'

I pointed her at a waiter with a tray of oyster canapés and as she helped herself – two, three, four shovelled straight down – I made my escape. In relief I drank the wine I was left holding. After so long on the wagon, what was one glass?

Truefitt was more than a bit drunk. We grinned at each other and he mentioned not drinking with glandular fever, which we thought very droll. It was by then too noisy for talk, so I parted a fed-up-looking waiter from his bottle of wine and made sure I poured myself the most. I felt good for the first time since arriving.

Then we were somewhere else, me and the woman in the pillbox hat, not dancing so much as clinging together like survivors of some terrible wreckage. There was deafening music and an enormous squash of people lurching under spangled lights. Nailed to one wall was a big fish in a glass case: a Robinsonian pike, I thought to myself. Then to the bar and more crowds and much shouting at an overworked man in a red waistcoat for more drinks. Doubles; what the hell. What was her name and what had I been on about? How had we got wherever we were, come to that? My balance was off.

'Great hat,' I managed by way of a safety shot.

'So you said.'

Perhaps not as drunk as she made out. 'Ah, you remember.' I tried changing the subject – not easy under the circumstances – and got started up again. She was a jiggly little thing, with an arse to match, not bad. She said, 'You are funny.'

'Why?'

'Asking if we're on a boat.' Had I?

She took me upstairs into the fresh air where it was cool and less crowded, and I saw that we were indeed in the middle of the Thames and passing what looked like Surrey Docks. Over the side railing, the water ran black below and seemed a long way down. I turned back and looked at her, thinking about the drunk couples Robinson and I used to trail. 'How did we get here?' I asked and she laughed her out-of-control laugh. I had the vaguest memory of a group from the other party coming on to this one, and an altercation with a taxi driver about the number of passengers allowed in a cab.

We went back downstairs and managed to get more drinks and a seat. The heat was crushing. There was a pay phone just behind us that a man was trying to use. He did a slow-motion drunk act trying to insert the coin, finally succeeded and accidentally sprayed the rest of his change all over the floor. I looked at the woman. She looked pale. I smiled. 'What?' she asked. I tried to explain that I was supposed to have glandular fever. Before I could elaborate she was wiping her mouth in alarm and emitting little chirrups of disgust and using what was left of her drink as a gargle. The man on the phone dropped the receiver, proved too drunk to collect it, so lurched on to all fours, where he knelt barking like a dog into the dangling mouthpiece. 'Listen,' I said to her, too bored to continue. 'Do you know Robinson?'

She went quite white and her gloved hand – I'd not noticed the glove before; had she just put it on? – flew to her mouth and she jack-knifed forward in her seat, as if stabbed in the back. There then followed the noise of a bucket being emptied as she heaved the best part of two dozen undigested oyster canapés on to the floor. Not that anyone paid any attention to this spectacular out-pouring. The man in the background continued barking, uninterrupted, and the rest of the party had degenerated into a drunken shambles. The whole room looked as though it were in the grip of a seizure.

She came up for air before another bout of vomiting. Her pillbox hat was askew. Tears of exertion in her eyes gave me a powerful urge to fuck her in the business of throwing up, plugging one end while the other spewed.

Perhaps she would let me in the toilet with her, but she wouldn't – 'Of course I'll be fucking all right' – so I stood around, helping myself to abandoned drinks, waiting for her to clean up.

A row of people sat swaying in the bar, hardly blinking when one keeled over, snapping backwards like a rotten tooth. Dancers careered out of control. Someone skidded and shot across the floor, taking at least three people down. The music was turned louder and couples crashed around like dodgem cars. I didn't feel so hot myself. Fuck it, one last brandy. There was some disagreement at the bar when it came to paying.

I woke up, cramped and uncomfortable, somewhere in the open. Flecks of rain fell from a grey sky. Had I imagined a pair of black Oxfords close by? Had he come? Had he wanted to fuck me as I'd wanted to her? I rolled over and groaned. Somewhere along the way I had been sick. I could smell it. What time was it? Ten something; it couldn't be. Then I remembered I still kept my watch run down, my one attachment to my days of truancy. I recognised that I was back in Soho, in a grimy doorway at the bottom end of Wardour Street, in the shadow of St Anne's. Back to square one. Soho: a state of mind, that crumbling time zone built up of absenteeism, dereliction, vagrancy and atheism. (I had sought out the irresponsible heart of the city.) For a long time I stared, helpless and incapable, at the church with its bombed-out body and surviving steeple. It was an appropriate landmark and symbol, I decided, for this other, less tangible realm.

Kneeling, propped against the bench in front, at the back of St Patrick's in Soho Square, open for early morning Mass – what day of the week was it? – I felt a bit less dead. The congregation, such as it was, stood up for the gospel. Afterwards, I'd catch a tube, though I doubted I were up to it. Another wave of nausea and I gave up standing, slumped back down to my knees and lay with my head in my arms and wondered where my wallet had gone. The priest, in green chasuble, raised the chalice, the server rang the bell, and the others in the congregation bowed their heads. After the first panic about the lost wallet subsided, I was surprised to find myself relieved and pleasantly giddy. Simple tastes from now on. Back on the wagon, get fit, maybe even start going to Mass.

Afterwards I felt sick again and had to lie down on a bench in Soho Square, until someone shook me awake. 'Well, old man. Certainly exceeded yourself this time.'

I groaned and stared at his shoes. They were as polished as ever. I asked how he'd known where to find me. He hadn't, he replied. He was passing by chance.

I stood up. 'Christ, I feel awful. I'm going to fall over.' Robinson steadied me and walked me slowly out of the gardens. He hailed a passing taxi. I wasn't sure I could manage a ride without being ill, but he said we weren't going far.

He took me to a flat in a large apartment block north of the BBC, up by the park. We took a rickety old lift with a folding metal grille. 'Nearly there,' said Robinson.

He unlocked the door to an apartment on the top floor, helped me down the corridor and into a narrow bedroom. When he saw I was incapable of undressing he helped me off with my clothes. The furniture in the room was heavy and dated, like in a prosperous old department store. There didn't seem to be anyone else about. Robinson told me to get some rest. 'You're all in.' I asked why he hadn't shown up at the party. 'You were gone by the time I got there.' I didn't believe him.

I woke in the dark, weak and shivering. The door was ajar. A slant of light shone in from the hall. My clothes were gone.

Robinson was in the kitchen. I shouted at him, accusing him of hiding my clothes to stop me from leaving. He looked amused. 'No need to throw a paddy, old man. Hungry, are we?'

I told him it was my clothes I wanted.

'Better get something in your stomach first, something light.'

I was easily persuaded back to bed. Robinson served chicken broth with plain bread and brought it in on an old tray with folding legs, then left straight away, like a nurse. I realised how hungry I was and drank from the bowl.

Afterwards I slept again, right through to the morning. Robinson was already up. He asked if I fancied coffee and eggs. 'Your clothes are in the bathroom,' he added.

They lay freshly laundered and pressed, wrapped in cellophane, like new. Over breakfast I apologised for my rudeness. We sat in comfortable silence, I looking out of the window at the mild grey sky while Robinson read the paper, sometimes aloud. Once he caught me looking at him and asked what it was. I told him I'd decided he didn't exist. He threw back his head and laughed. 'Who does, old man? Who does?'

He left around noon, saying that he would be back soon. 'Well, tomorrow morning at the latest. Make yourself at home.' He left a set of keys and demonstrated carefully how each lock worked, three of them altogether and another for the front of the building.

After he had gone I searched the flat for clues. Needles. Pills. Nothing would have surprised me, not that I really expected to discover anything beyond the absence of any serious trace of him that I did find. There were just a few ordered possessions: a row of books, all paperback, forgettable thrillers apart from a copy of De Quincey's *Confessions of an English Opium Eater*, and, in a wardrobe, a spare pair of black Oxfords and Robinson's winter coat. I thought of those shiny black shoes, the moon face and the secrets he carried. Though he had not been long gone, I could not picture him clearly.

After three days, during which the phone did not ring and I reported the loss of my wallet and credit cards, and read my way through some of Robinson's thrillers, there was still no sign of him. By then the fridge, far from being full to begin with, was empty. I let myself out of the apartment and, as I had no money, walked home and arrived to find my wife in the process of leaving.

She told me she was going back to Boston, to a post where the annual salary was more than double mine, and I was not to go with her.

After she left I saw how much our marriage, which was in its third year of attrition, meant to me. I recognised too how little I had given in return. We had both turned corners – or so I thought before her departure – that required coming to terms with the fact neither of us would achieve the effortless success of which we had once dreamed. In as much as we spent our time cauterising each other's frayed nerves, ours was a technically clinical relationship. I missed her.

Looking now at how I have organised these experiences into some sort of progression I see the order is only approximate. This journey or voyage, as I came to regard it, had none of the convenience of a story, but jumped in fits and starts, blurred and fell apart as surely as I did. The movement was one of uncertain descent, I knew that quite early on, but events I connect as part of some cause and emotional effect probably happened further apart. I associate the dwarf in the porno cinema with the day I stole the wallet from the man in glasses, but now wonder if the dwarf didn't come earlier. And the nights at the office were perhaps fewer. There was a semblance of domestic life to which I have not referred, clung to more than I care to admit. Anxieties that seem clear now were not obvious then. The person I lie to best is myself.

The house sold well. I paid off the mortgage and split the not inconsiderable amount left with my wife. My share remained in an ordinary bank account, which felt right for my lack of interest in continuing to organise my existence in the usual ways.

I looked at a few flats, all bodged conversions in dreary Victorian terraces with three or four dustbins outside in their own little sentry boxes. This was not what I'd imagined for myself: not much more than a bedsit in some outer suburb where I saw myself standing alone at the back window on a summer's evening, watching the pasty couple downstairs enjoy their garden rights for the hour or so the sun penetrated as far as their undernourished little basement lawn.

I was on the point of buying the last flat I looked at (a couple sat in the garden; I watched them go inside). The young estate agent was smug, had been taught to recognise the condition of his clients and the sign around my neck clearly read: fucked-up. The boxy rooms had thin walls of cheap plasterboard, and sound travelled: the noise of sex being hastily taken came up clearly from downstairs. The estate agent's smirk lost him his sale.

I wandered into another room, opened the window and inspected the sill. There was rot in the frame, nothing serious, but rot none the less and it occurred to me I'd built a life for myself on insubstantial foundations, and that even the most cursory inspection of my own cellar, which I'd not gone down into for too long, would reveal how rotten. Downstairs the keening reached a peak.

I moved around, staying here and there in spare rooms, minding empty flats while owners were away: a network of precarious solitary lives. In between I moved into a small hotel in Frith Street. I took long baths, wasted time in cafes, pretending to take an interest in the newspapers, before returning for an afternoon rest. Then, putting on a fresh shirt for the evening, I went out and ate alone. During these periods of sober indulgence I never made plans to meet anyone. Instead I treated the city as though it were foreign, avoiding old haunts and going where tourists went. Evenings usually ended with a visit to one of the big cinemas around Leicester Square to watch a Hollywood movie, chosen on impulse. I tried to avoid discovering the title of the film until it came up on the screen. Going with such an empty mind, I was rarely disappointed. Back at the hotel I read late into the night, burrowed down in clean white sheets. It was the respectable alternative to my previous life in Soho.

I went back to work again, this time cutting film, which was how I'd started out. The job involved nothing more than splicing together news material, enough to keep my hands and mind occupied for hours at a stretch. I was back in Soho for this, not that I really noticed. From 8.30 in the morning until after seven in the evening I sat in a darkened little room running the Steenbeck back and forward.

What remained of any personal life was spent getting rid of things – books, clothes, records and the rest of the accumulated junk. The little worth keeping I put in store. The rest fitted into three large suitcases that got lugged around and gradually reduced to one. During one of these clearing sessions I came across the keys to Robinson's apartment.

All I could remember was that the flat lay in an anonymous stretch of blocks somewhere north of Portland Place, in a residential area with little sign of residence. The occasional family got in and out of cars with diplomatic plates, and there was the odd shop run by Indians, open all hours, Sundays too. It was an area where it always felt like Sunday, full of discretion and aimlessness. Clocks ran slower there. No wonder Robinson made a point of staying out late.

Twice I failed to find the apartment. At the third attempt I stopped work early and left just before dusk. It began to spit with rain as I crossed Oxford Street and the first lights were coming on. By the time I found what I thought was Robinson's block the streets were wet and a steady drizzle fell. The front doors were open and the hall, with its dark mahogany panels, faded pattern carpet, brass stair-rods and expensive musty smell seemed more familiar than other buildings I had tried. The lift in its heavy wire cage and awkward grille-gates were as I remembered. When I'd left the last time, an over-rouged old woman had been stuck inside with her yapping poodle. She called out in a voice used to giving orders, 'Don't just walk off. Do something.'

Robinson's flat was on the top floor straight ahead of the lift. The keys – Yale, mortise and Chubb – all worked. I stepped inside. This arrival felt like a home-coming, an odd sensation as I had taken in so little before and what I remembered of the place I did not par-ticularly like.

The apartment was the mansion type with heavy doors and a long, dark corridor with rooms off, one side overlooking the street, the other an interior well. Robin-son once told me the place was owned by a Jewish businessman who had passed it on to a son now in America. The story fitted the expensive Fifties furniture, bought for comfort rather than taste, the old wall-lights like candelabra and an overall effect of unfashionable upholstered opulence.

The anonymity of it all made me wonder if I were in the right place, until I recognised the old kitchen refri-gerator, the size of a small wardrobe, and the scuffed black and white linoleum floor tiles. A cup stood on the draining board where I had left it. No one had been there since.

I took to visiting once or twice a week for an hour or so, and sometimes staying the night. The place remained empty and untouched, though I fancied I saw the smal-lest traces of disturbance in the gathering dust. My vanity was hurt because I could find no message from Robinson, some private communication, intelligible only to myself, saying where he was.

On a damp, warm evening at the end of October, I knew as I crossed the threshold that something was dif-ferent. The mustiness still lingered, but there were other faint smells, a trace of dark tobacco. In the sitting room, curtains previously open were drawn. Armchairs had been pushed against the wall, leaving lighter patches on the carpet. The weight of the silence stopped me calling out.

In the kitchen a saucer of milk stood on the floor, and around the rim of another (white china with a blue band that I associated with such flats) lay the shit-like crusted remains of what looked like cat food. A large fly fed off it. I was startled by the loud hum of the fridge starting up. The fly buzzed noisily against the closed slats of the venetian blind. I went to open the fridge and stopped, nervous of what might be in there. (Flesh shining stickily under the fridge's interior light.)

The fly buzzed around, following.

The bathroom floor was wet. A piece of rubber hose lay on the black and white tiles like an exhibit in a catalogue of improvised tortures. The bath was full of dirty grey water gone cold.

I moved silently down the corridor. Through the crack of a bedroom door I saw the corner of a mattress, and a bare, pale foot.

Two naked bodies lay on the bed, both dead white and dead still. When the fly settled on one, it didn't move. There was no sign of violence.

I slipped out and went to Robinson's room.

I shared the flat with this strange, grave couple, who were so alike and in tune that I wondered if they were brother and sister. They were young, thin and androgynous, with long, boyish hair of identical black, and smooth bodies. Both wore kohl around their eyes. They showed no curiosity at finding me there, never made a noise and rarely spoke, communicating by secretive smiles. Their time was spent entirely indoors, almost always naked, about which they were quite unselfconscious. Mostly they fucked – though the word is too unceremonial for their solemn, dreamy ritual. It was not unusual to find them coupled on the floor of the hall, never starting or finishing, always just languidly, and imaginatively, joined, rarely in the same position twice. Mine was the only door ever closed. I watched her peeing once, while he sat on the edge of the bath. Another time, I found her – none of us had got around to exchanging names – squatting over a saucer of milk, put out for the cat, and bathing her vulva. 'I'm feeding pussy,' she said in a distant voice. (They were like cats and I even grew fond of them. As for the cat proper, it was a visitor from another apartment and made its way along the parapet to the kitchen window.) She regarded me with her incurious, unblinking gaze. 'He said you might come.'

'Who did?'

'Ross.'

'Who's Ross? You mean Robinson?'

She shrugged. 'He said you had keys.' I asked again if Ross were Robinson. She chipped a flake of paint off the skirting surround with her fingernail and did not answer.

'What else did he say?'

'He said you were to have his room.'

'What does Ross look like? Is he tall?'

She got up and stood awkwardly. 'I must go now,' she whispered. I gripped her arm, wanting to know more. I was not aware of the boy behind me until he said, 'He always uses the telephone.'

The days grew shorter without my noticing. The weather was strange and unpredictable like a hangover that catches one unawares. I started to wear Robinson's long overcoat, though it was too large. I worked ten or eleven hours a day and went back at night after stopping for something to eat, sometimes buying a tin of food for the cat, which was with us most of the time. I liked walking home in the dark, past the lighted windows.

In Robinson's room, now mine, there was an empty secretaire which I imagined full of papers that would tell me about him, things too that I had no wish to know, like his real opinion of me.

At night I read or watched the old black and white television, housed in a large cabinet behind double doors. Sometimes the couple sat on the floor, dressed, perhaps out of deference to me, in baggy jerseys. I learned to be comfortable with their silences.

For days at a stretch I'd not see them, though I knew they were in for the simple reason that they never went out. Sometimes one of them asked me to bring something back, usually chocolate, for which they paid in advance with money kept in a tin. The fridge was always empty, apart from some basics. The business of cooking did not fit with the silent, entombed atmosphere of the apartment. Once I invited them out for a meal but they declined. During the day the curtains stayed drawn. Mine were the only ones ever open. Then I too left them closed.

At night I woke up to find them immobile at the foot of my bed, weird guardian angels. I was reassured by their statue-like presence, watching over me. Perhaps I should have been afraid.

Their drug habit was as unselfconscious as everything else they did. (Whether these drugs were delivered or collected I had no idea.) While they smoked I read to them from Robinson's battered old copy of De Quincey and told them how he first took opium, bought from a chemist in Oxford Street, and how he lived at the top of Greek Street where a bank now stood, in a gloomy, deserted house where his only companion, apart from the rats, was a girl of ten who asked him to protect her from the ghosts she feared.

49

Like De Quincey, I first took the drug one wet Sunday afternoon, though not for rheumatic fever as he had, rather from a curiosity provoked by the couple's blank, dreamy expressions. 'A duller spectacle this earth of ours has not to show than a rainy Sunday in London,' he wrote before losing himself in 'the abyss of divine enjoyment'.

The drug insulated us even more within the comfortable bubble we had made for ourselves. The strange cocktail of cutting film (unreal enough in itself), moderate amounts of alcohol and a pipe in the evening removed me entirely from the exterior world. Nights passed in the grip of a euphoric insomnia, interspersed with cat-naps of profound depth from which I awoke fully refreshed.

De Quincey's little 'companion in wretchedness' took to sleeping curled in the corner of my room. I thought she was a fantasy until I heard her with the vacuum cleaner (none of us ever cleaned) in the middle of the day. I showed the tracks of the Hoover on the carpet to the couple as proof.

Strangers started to stay, a night or so at a time, and for a while there was a traffic of sorts. The arrival of these men – always men – was announced to me either by note or a whispered aside from one of the couple. They never stayed more than once, except the one I thought of as the Dutchman, who came four times at most. Beyond a nod of acknowledgement, I had nothing to do with these tough-looking visitors whose self-possession made us seem so fragile. The couple's door stayed closed until we were alone again. The feeling afterwards was one of relief.

I wondered if Robinson knew of these movements, perhaps controlled them. It didn't take much to work out that the place was some sort of safe-house.

The drug dreams started to fork. Early peaceful images receded, as if scribbled over by an impatient malevolence. The apartment started to break up and I watched darkness pour out of hair-line cracks in the plaster. There was machinery somewhere too, a ruthless hum of efficient cogs, levers, pulleys and weights that shifted the walls. The couple heard it too when I pointed it out, and we tried to locate the source without success. By imperceptible degrees the hall grew narrower, became neglected and dank, until I was cut off. The apartment was a series of chasms whose only exits were sheer precipices above giddy voids. The path to the couple's room became too narrow to pass and I found it impossible to turn back. I was trapped, immured. The terrible buzzing in my ears was more than the rushing blood of panic, it was the inexorable whirr of a deadly, ancient machinery closing the walls.

Doors previously open became shut. One hid a rat the size of a car into which I saw the last of the cat disappearing. Behind another lay the green, spumescent ocean of my worst nightmare.

One rainy evening, as I was about to have a pipe, the bell rang. Thinking it one of the usual occasional visitors, I answered without hiding anything. The man in the doorway was tall and his mackintosh wet. He held up a laminated card showing he was a policeman. He knew my name.

We stood in the hall. His hair was slick with rain. He wanted to know about Robinson. Did I know him? When had I last seen him? Was he a close friend? Where was he? This bizarre drawing-room play into which I was plunged unrehearsed and without lines was the stuff of surreal dreams. Some automatic reflex provided the answers. Robinson lived and worked abroad, had done for years, somewhere in the Middle East, I had last heard. He was in London very infrequently, he was no more than an acquaintance. At the back of my mind, I had expected something like this.

Then, prefaced by a routine apology for being the bearer of bad news, he went on to say that he thought Robinson was dead.

A body had been washed up by the river after being in the water a long time. Nothing was suspected and what remained was the formal but tricky matter of identification. The corpse was in an advanced state of decay.

'Nasty at the best of times, drownings.' He wanted me to view the body, in the absence of any next of kin.

I said, 'I hardly knew him. I'm not sure I'd recognise him. If the body's as bad as you say.' I wondered how the policeman's investigation had led him to the apartment and to me, given a lack of obvious connection.

'I can appreciate your reluctance, sir,' (sir!) he said.

'Yours was the only name we found among what was left of Mr Robinson's possessions. That and this address. And a foreign credit card in his name. Oh, and a wallet.'

After the policeman had gone, I lay on my bed and smoked, listening to the storm build while trying to decide whether this was one of Robinson's jokes or if he really had been tipped into the Thames. Neither would have surprised me.

The storm grew in intensity through the night, lashing the windows of the room with such force that I feared the glass would smash. I went to inspect. Beyond the glass I could see nothing, only black, no lights, nothing. I told myself, as I reached for the window, that there was no such thing as total darkness. The handle was torn from my grasp by the wind. The roar of the gale was deafening. Then the whole room started to pitch and heave. Furniture toppled and the bed crashed into me and drove me against the far wall.

I crawled to the door. Beyond it lay the ocean of my nightmare. Vast waves ran green to black in the dark. Not another soul was on board. The deck yawned and dropped into the path of a huge wave. My scream was lost as the wave smashed down and drove the wind from my body. Sliding away towards the edge, my hand locked on something. It was the cross-hatching of a wooden raft and, with the last of my strength, I lashed myself to it. (A memory from another life: Robinson, drunk, his vision narrowed to a few scattered drinks on a bar top, as though trying to divine in their configuration some secret pattern.) Tarred cracks between planks. Joins in the raft. A remnant of tarpaulin. Spume racing down the deck. By an enormous willing of the continued existence of these intimate details I told myself I could abate the fury of the storm.

A deeper noise, a sucking roar, broke my concentration, then blackness, and the end surely, but no. Only a greater isolation: spreadeagled on the raft as it climbed a sheer wall of water – taller than a house – terrifying in itself but nothing to what lay above. The fragile raft teetered on the top of the giddy slide down to the foot of the next waiting wave, and an immense, tumultuous sea lay revealed in the coming dawn, above it a racing sky of black clouds. All lay mocked by a tiny patch of distant blue and the bloodiest of sunrises. For what?

I swore never again, a resolution immediately forgotten after my trip to the mortuary, and I was back again in the 'depths below depths' encountered by De Quincey, 'from which it seemed hopeless that I could ever re-ascend'.

The corpse belonged to those depths. More disturbing than its jellied eyes, bloated head and cod-grey skin, long since separated from the bone beneath, was the profound silence given off by the body.

The sounds of the identification, more than this vision of such hideous distension, were the hardest to expel from my mind afterwards – the rasp of wheels on the metal box, like an extended filing cabinet, which held the body, the hum of fluoride light, the whisper of the sheet as the face became revealed. I looked, swayed but did not faint as I had feared.

In another room, they sat me down with a glass of water poured from a tap with a sinister, blade-like handle. I asked why the handle was like that. So it could be turned on and off with the elbow when the user's hands were bloody, came the laconic reply.

I confirmed that what I had seen had once been Robinson and was his corpse. I inspected his final possessions, including his wallet, which I had given him after stealing it from the man with glasses. The leather had lost all its colour and the wallet itself was almost unrecognisable. I was asked if I wanted to take any of these meagre belongings. 'What for?' I said. 'They're no use to me.'

AFTER

I saw a tattered labyrinth (it was London).
Jorge Luis Borges

The dog stops barking after Robinson has gone.
Weldon Kees, 'Robinson'

DEATH BY DROWNING became Robinson. I associated him with water, because of his description of Soho as a rat-run, with its suggestion of ships. During the wrecked nights following what I came to think of as the Day of Identification, I fancied I saw schooners moored in the streets of Soho, masts higher than the rooftops, a harbour in the square, the streets running off it backwater creeks. Sometimes Soho was the ship itself, sometimes the raft to which I clung after being swept overboard. (Oxford Street a tidal wave poised to sweep everything before it.) Approached from Robinson's apartment, from the dead land to the north, it was like stepping aboard from a jetty; underfoot a swell that required the rolling gait of a sailor; several beers later, the heave more pronounced, choppy seas.

It was not Robinson in the mortuary. Of course, I had not really expected it to be. It might have been but it was not, and more than once in the days following I shouted, 'Fuck Robinson!' Fuck him for knowing I would be his witness.

Nothing happened, I didn't expect it to. One day the couple were gone, moved on, the drug supply with them. I sweated the stuff out of my system by taking long walks, pushing myself out to Hampstead and beyond – Burnt Oak, Colindale, the Welsh Harp, old stamping grounds. No one came to the apartment any more.

I moved jobs (I was done with editing) and got fixed up with work in an office, selling advertising space over the telephone, very respectable. I carried an attaché case (with nothing inside) to show how respectable. I tried very hard to take an interest in others, daydreamed during working hours and cheated when filling in work cards listing calls made, but so did everyone else. I took care not to walk too close to the edge, and, going home along Oxford Street, stuck to the north side.

Occasionally, I thought about Robinson navigating his way, a long voyager, looking different too, his shoes the only clue to his former self; black leather on varnished deck wood. They would be his undoing; slippery soles would pitch him overboard. Shoes that would be kicked off, while Robinson trod water, then swam a patient crawl until exhausted before rolling on his back and letting the sea take him.

As a test of nerve I went back one night to the bars where I was once a regular. I was not recognised or, if I were, no one joined me. I ate a bit and drank a little and remembered what this drinking business did. It cleared a space for a while. I had a last drink and went on to a place where I could get another, then called it a night. There was no attraction left in the bottle and I knew I needn't fear it any more.

I walked under the arch at Manette Street, this time

checking out for good, and down to Leicester Square for the late-night movies. By the tube station the street was busy with cocky lads and girls with streaked hair, up for a night out. The usual crowd of beggars hung around, mainly pasty kids, sitting in doorways in sleeping bags. Like most people, I had learned to ignore them. I brushed aside an outstretched hand in the thick of the crowd, then some instinct made me turn and look back. I fancied it was Robinson, scruffy and unshaven, moving away. I was too surprised to call after him.

I dreamed again of Robinson's shoes, scuffed and neglected, soles worn thin. He had not struck out, after all, but had submerged himself instead, sunk without trace. This descent was puzzling: surely his vanity would not permit such personal deterioration. On the other hand, it could have been premeditated, a deliberate letting go, truancy expanding into vagrancy.

I appropriated the old Robinson in his absence. My squatting in the apartment and identification of the corpse gave me, I felt, the right to purchase his character. I speculated about him, like an actor getting to grips with a part. I understood the element of self-dramatisation in Robinson, and was sure that his latest descent had its emotional plumb-line. Robinson was nothing if not true to the parts he chose to play. He had moved on to another role in whatever movie it was that lay spooled in his head.

In the end he called, as I knew he would. Four on Saturday we agreed, then the familiar revision: 'Let's say fifteen minutes later. You don't mind, do you, old man?' Then he added, 'I can rely on you, can't I?' I wondered if this was an oblique reference to what he had put me through.

I was late and paused at the top of the steps by

Charing Cross Station, above Villiers Street. Robinson was waiting, halfway down. He turned towards me and, as he did, I stepped back out of sight. I stood there, jostled by the crowd hurrying into the underground, Robinson a hundred yards away in the chasm of Villiers Street, and beyond him the river, choppy brown, the river in which he was supposed to have drowned. Spring would come before too long. Robinson was in an overcoat, looking smart. (It could not have been him I thought I saw begging.) Then he saw me and his hand went up in greeting. The frankness of his smile was obvious even at that distance. He strode forward, gloved fist smacking palm.

Some detail of that afternoon escapes me, some little trick pulled off by Robinson. The unexpected shaking of hands, perhaps, like some foreigner imitating what he thinks is the English way. The direct gaze. The smile. The inquiry after my health. 'You look weary, old man.' Banal remarks about the weather. I had rehearsed this meeting, intending to take the initiative, but he was the one who looked me up and down for an explanation.

'What's been going on?' he asked, all innocence. He took my arm, asked if I was hungry. I wasn't, but we went to eat anyway, in a steak house where a private conversation was difficult. The place was full, even so late in the afternoon, with tired-looking tourists in anoraks and students with rucksacks and inflated trainers.

I asked Robinson where he had been. 'Abroad,' he replied, vaguely. I told him he was meant to be dead. His double-take was faultless.

'Astonishing,' was all he said after I finished.

His coolness angered me. I reached over and grasped his wrist. The familiar look, letting me know I'd been drawn. Dusk fell on the Strand.

I let go. Robinson swilled some wine, then told me what he had been up to, as though this might provide an explanation. He had been going back and forth to Hamburg.

I listened dully. The meal was to his advantage. Our meeting was no longer about my curiosity but his appetite. His business had not been going well. He was taking stock, transferring assets and relocating. 'I've got a proposition that might interest you,' he said between mouthfuls. 'Not now. Later,' he said when I asked what. He pushed his empty plate aside, leaned forward and announced his plan to become rich.

'I thought you already were.'

'Not seriously.' His had always been a cash economy, his deals determined by whom he could buy from and sell to. He explained how dealing worked, how it depended on demand and on contacts. Having the supply without the contacts was as useless as having no supply. 'There's a pecking order to such things. A protocol.' I asked exactly what it was that he dealt in. The ironic smile. 'Oh, I know what you're thinking. I credited you with more imagination.' He reached into his pocket. 'Here, I've something to show you.'

It was a photograph torn from a magazine, showing a large and exultant crowd watching the Berlin Wall coming down. I looked at Robinson, not sure what I was meant to say. He smiled his secretive smile. 'The harder something is to get,' he murmured, 'the more people want it. The Wall was good to me. I was sorry to see it go.'

Robinson smuggled art out of Eastern Europe, buying cheap for dollars (worth a fortune locally) and selling at a high profit in the West. 'I was surprised we got away with it for so long.'

I assumed he was talking about icons and other religious art, for which there was a market in the West, but he shook his head, saying there was too much competition. The black market for them was too well known and therefore open to infiltration by the authorities.

I looked at the photograph again, wondering why Robinson made a point of carrying it. Then I saw. I was surprised I'd not spotted him before. In the crowd of uplifted, joyous faces, his was the only preoccupied one, looking down.

Robinson suggested we walk over to the Marquis of Granby as it was early enough for it not to be crowded. The waitress was slow to bring the bill. He stood up impatiently. 'Come on,' he said, daring me to walk out without paying. He left and I started to follow, lost my nerve and went back. Robinson waited outside. 'Blessed are the meek,' he said, contemplating his toe-caps. 'The drinks are on you too, I'm afraid. A temporary cash flow problem.'

'Lost your wallet?' I asked, trying to give my voice an edge. Robinson caught my drift, and laughed unexpectedly. 'It's the damnedest thing, but I have.'

The corpse on the slab came back to me in a rush, and with it the ghost of a moment in Old Compton Street, the abrupt end to our first meeting. 'Fuck you,' I said and walked off.

I went down into the underground. There was a train just leaving. I expected to see Robinson following, jumping aboard as the doors closed.

Instead, he was there at the next station (he had been in another carriage), serious and contrite as he came and sat down. He had it all figured out. 'I know what you're thinking,' he said. I had to lean closer to hear him. His breath smelt of wine. He talked about the wallet, and how I associated him with not carrying one, let alone any identification, and yet the body pulled from the river had both.

I nodded warily, not looking at him. We travelled in silence during the interminable stretch between Baker Street and St John's Wood. 'What do you think I am?' he said at last, emphasising the space between each word. I looked at him. There were tears in his eyes, to my surprise.

We got off at Kilburn. I needed a drink. We went into a crowded Irish pub on the High Road, full of hard-faced men with pale eyes and white skins, and accents that chopped at words as though they were a source of mistrust. The place had a mean feel, and Robinson was silent. He downed his beer quickly, and said provocatively, loud enough to be heard, 'If there's one thing I can't stand it's a room full of Micks.' A drunken man nearby gave us a slurred look in slow motion before going back to contemplating his stout.

I hustled Robinson out, and took off down the High Road at a pace, fearful that a posse would follow. Robinson was amused by my fright. I found his fearlessness stupid. 'And if some big Paddy had called your bluff?'

'Ah, Micks come cheap. I'd have made light of it and bought him a drink.'

I'd no intention of staying in Kilburn so we walked down the dirty brown torrent of the High Road and over to St John's Wood, crossing the boundary that separated urban meanness from sedate, inner-suburban prosperity. The streets became deserted and calm, clean too, with none of the rolling, empty beer cans and discarded fast-food boxes of a few hundred yards back.

We stopped at the Clifton, but Robinson didn't like its ersatz Bohemian atmosphere and wanted to move on. 'Christ, you're spoiling for a fight,' I said in exasperation. This drew a laugh. 'I'm just looking to get comfortable,' he replied.

We ended up in an enormous barn of a pub at the far end of Hamilton Terrace, done out like a Bavarian hunting lodge. There, over countless beers chased with whisky, I finally managed to extract some sort of biography from him. He elaborated on his profitable line in East European art dealing.

The idea had come from meeting an East German artist in England on a cultural exchange and Robinson had driven across to Leipzig later that summer. He returned with three canvases hidden in the roof of his car, which he sold on at a mark-up of five hundred per cent. Later, as his profits rose, he paid others to smuggle the stuff out. Just like Robinson, I thought, to rob the poor to rob the rich. He must have read my mind because he shrugged, and said the artists were paid in hard currency, well enough by their standards.

With the fall of the Berlin Wall, Robinson lost interest. 'There were whole convoys going east. And the artists got greedy. It was no fun any more.' What he told me fitted with his secretive image, and, important for him, avoided the predictable.

I'd lost count of how much we had drunk. I'd paid for every round. There wasn't money left for many more, and we had reached the stage of drinking fast. I got us a last beer and whisky, and tried to focus on Robinson. Between his recent trips to Hamburg, he had taken to walking the city by night, always pushing east. He was bored with the smart set and their noisy, mediocre clubs. I heard his metal heels clicking on empty pavements, saw him standing in a doorway, squinting up at fine rain lit by a street lamp, and wondered if there were some connection between my own retreat during this time and his nocturnal wanderings.

He borrowed a damp, empty room in Hackney from a book dealer, sometimes staying there and sometimes sleeping rough. 'I wanted another perspective.'

At last we got to the business of the wallet. Robinson had hung on to it after he'd offered it back to me. 'For sentimental reasons.' (An ironic eyebrow.) He had even started to keep things in it, he said, but somewhere along the way it had got stolen or lost, picked up perhaps by the man on whom it was found.

'So,' said Robinson, 'I'm officially dead.' He looked pleased with the idea. 'One thing puzzles me. Why did you say it was me?' Disingenuous to the last, I thought.

'Because I rather hoped it was.'

'Touché, old man.'

Robinson was hungry again so we had to find a cash machine for me to get more money. We went to a late-night cafe on the Edgware Road where I dozed drunkenly while he ate a huge greasy meal.

We parted on the street with Robinson saying he'd be in touch and reminding me he had a proposition. I'd forgotten. 'Just an idea,' he said vaguely, looking like the Robinson of old. Feeling maudlin by then, I told him I was glad to see him again and was up for any entertainment on offer.

'Oh by the way,' he said as his parting shot, 'some people know me as Ross these days.'

'Yes. I know,' I replied, hoping to surprise him.

'Good. Just so you know.'

We were both playing it pretty cool. 'So long, old man.' Robinson hands in pockets of his smart overcoat. Me in his old one, curiously unremarked upon by Robinson.

The proposition was a disappointment. I thought Robinson miscalculated the timing of his offer, just after I'd been given a supervisory position at the telephone sales company.

'Interesting work, old man?' My empty attaché case lay on the table between us. I shrugged. There was a pay rise which would make my salary a lot more than what Robinson was proposing.

Robinson wanted me to run a bookshop, his bookshop. 'I won it in a bet,' he said, offering no further explanation. I told him I couldn't see myself working in a bookshop. He explained patiently that I would have the place to myself. It was exclusive and well located – just around the corner from the pub we were in – and specialised in rare books.

'What do you mean, it's your bookshop?'

'I told you, I won it. In a game of cards.' The previous owner had been a compulsive gambler, he added. I told him I could have worked that out for myself.

'Besides,' he went on lightly. 'What else have you got? You've fucked up your career, and don't tell me that supervising telephone sales counts for anything. You've fucked up your marriage. You drink too much.' He finished his beer and tapped the empty glass lightly on the table.

'Why me?' I asked. I was looking for more to fill up the day than opening a shop, collecting a bit of money and locking up.

He grew serious. 'I want someone I can trust.' He persuaded me at least to look at the place as it was only two minutes away.

The shop stood in an alley running off St Martin's Lane, not the one where most of the second-hand book dealers were. I was expecting a fusty room full of old leather-bound volumes of interest only to the most eccentric and esoteric. Instead, there was a bright space with a modern feel. I looked around. Nice desk. Telephone. Expensive rug on parquet flooring, cut flowers in a vase even, what was probably a pleasant view out of the window by day, out on to the traffic-free street. It was not really like a bookshop at all, and hard to imagine it being disturbed by anything so vulgar as customers. A single bureau bookcase was devoted to antiquarian books. The rest of the display was discreet and almost insolently infrequent, designed to show off elegant dust-wrappers to best advantage. I opened a book by a writer I did not know.

'Two hundred and fifty quid!' I looked at Robinson in astonishment. He glanced at the book and told me it had been banned and withdrawn from circulation soon after publication. He pulled out a neatly typed card that said as much.

'Do the job well and I'll get you a secretary and you can neck with her in the stack rooms.' These basement rooms contained several thousand well-kept, highly priced books, neatly shelved. At the front, the room extended under the pavement. Frosted glass cubes were set in to the ceiling to let in light. I thought about the pleasing shadows people walking above would make during the day.

It was the first place I had felt comfortable in since the office attic. It was the sign on the door that decided it; *Back in five minutes.* Or perhaps not. 'I thought you'd like that,' said Robinson, pleased.

I also liked the old-fashioned bell on the door that rang to announce a customer, not that there were many. The prices discouraged casual buyers, and the smartness of the shop intimidated the scruffy bargain hunters who cruised the bookshops in the Charing Cross Road. When it rained the place tended to fill up, though with no increase to sales. What regular clientele there was reminded me of the porno cinema audiences, less in appearance than for their dedication. Each sale I religiously entered in long-hand in a ledger. Some days the amount came to no more than a hundred pounds, three or four books at most.

When Robinson delivered new stock I spent busyish mornings in the basement unpacking and rearranging, and protecting the books' covers with cellophane. Pricing was done by a dealer of Robinson's acquaintance. Most of the business was done by mail order catalogue. Soon I was going down to the Trafalgar Square post office two or three times a day to send off parcels. Pulling down the dark green blind on the half-glass door of the shop and hanging up the five minute sign became one of life's small pleasures.

I moved the downstairs table into the recess directly under the pavement skylight so I could feel the movement of the pedestrians overhead, some of whom paused to look in the shop window. From the desk upstairs it was possible to spy on these window-shoppers from behind the window display. To improve the view on to the street I reduced the number of books in the window, leaving only the most expensive. This view was at its best, and most set-like, around dusk in the rain with umbrellas hurrying past. In the shop itself, in its details and fittings and situation, I found a rare harmony.

It was not an unhappy time. The regularity of the work helped: order, invoice and despatch, neat columns of marching figures, a sense of custody. I thought of it as a period of recuperation – a retreat from the world to take stock – though, looking back, I wonder if I was not undergoing some sort of crack-up. I made an inventory of lost possessions, emotional attachments, insults. At the same time, I thought of life as having achieved some sort of constancy, immunity even. I set aside five cigarettes for each day and restricted drinking to weekends, apart from an occasional beer. I walked everywhere for exercise. The lassitude that had previously washed over the afternoons vanished.

My own little personal gains stood in contrast to the dramatic upheavals read about in the papers – revolution, recession, stock-market crash, murder, epidemic, famine, aeroplanes falling out of the sky. Against this background of disaster – a collage that I checked on daily – my own life became curiously effortless.

Robinson receded in importance. He telephoned occasionally, usually from Hamburg. Sometimes a month passed between meetings. It struck me that he was putting on a lot of weight and often looked tired. One lunchtime we went across the way to the pub. He made no comment when I drank orange juice and listened politely to my little stories about the shop. I was privately relieved that he seemed bored with my small world.

Though I rarely went to the pub we were in, it felt like part of my patch, which gave me an advantage, an impression reinforced when a couple of other shop-keepers from the court paused to talk. They worked opposite me and dealt in photographs. The younger one did mornings, her older friend took over after lunch. In appearance they were vaguely Bohemian and I wondered if they were lesbians. They often turned up for work in men's jackets. The older one was the jollier and treated running a shop as a joke. Her laughter often drifted across the court, prompting me to wonder if I had given up fucking along with everything else.

Some mornings I caught myself watching the younger one. She had slim wrists and delicate hands and I preferred it when she wore her hair up to show her erotic neck to advantage.

Joan, the older one, had been first to introduce herself, soon after I moved in. She came across, eager for gossip about the previous owner and was so frankly curious that it was impossible to dislike her. She knew far more than I did. It turned out he had killed himself not long before – blown his brains out in front of a mirror. She didn't know why. I wondered if Robinson knew.

Joan was easy and chatty. She had a comfortable bosom, and sometimes I fantasised about her though not as much as I did over Veronica, the quieter friend. The few times I went over in the morning, I was made aware of Veronica's defensiveness. Her lack of small talk, I put down to indifference. She told me she had three children, which was why she worked mornings only. The children's father had been gone some time, and she and Joan lived together at the top of an enormous ramshackle house in Paddington, the rest of which was divided into bedsits. Veronica was about thirty, and a photographer without the time to practise. Most of this I gathered from afternoon cups of coffee with Joan, whose own private life was spent on the ricochet from one unreliable artist to another.

Robinson showed no particular interest in either when I introduced them in the pub. I was glad because I was starting to feel protective of the life I was building, and wanted to keep him out of it. After Joan and Veronica left, I watched him popping peanuts into his mouth. When he was done he tore the packet down the sides with a careful, childlike concentration and licked up the salt with his finger. He caught me watching and gave a shy, charming smile.

Before we parted I asked him if he knew what had happened to the previous owner of the shop. He didn't, and claimed not to have heard about the suicide. 'I didn't know that,' he said simply.

One morning Robinson was at the shop when I arrived and I had the impression he had been there all night, perhaps was sleeping there, a repeat of my office performance.

He was in the middle of eating a sandwich. Robinson was definitely putting on weight. His shirt was starting to strain at his belly. What looked like accounts lay scattered on the table. He flipped them closed. 'All right, old man? I'm just finishing.' Robinson the industrious, Robinson at his books, was a new one on me.

Since I'd last seen him, he had cut his hair short, almost to a crewcut, so that it looked like iron filings under a magnetic spell. He hadn't shaved in the meantime. His beard was light and scraggy, in contrast to his thick head of hair. With all his trips to Hamburg, Robinson was taking on a Germanic appearance. Heavy corduroy trousers with wide braces, a white shirt of heavy cotton, and stout Continental brogues with storm welts. I looked around, expecting to see the picture completed by a loden coat hanging on the door. Instead there was a belted green leather jacket, equally German. He had taken up smoking too, coarse, dangerous-looking cheroots that left a heavy smell. 'Two or three a day, that's all. By the way, old man, the flat you're in, the fellow that usually lives there, I spoke to him the other day.'

The gist of it was he was coming back and I had to leave. This was not a cause for regret. In fact, it suited my plans quite well. Joan had said one of the lodgers in her house wanted to sub-let for a year while she went to India on a research grant. I was tired of living alone, and also fancied insinuating my way into Veronica's life, albeit on a platonic level. I saw us eating spaghetti suppers around a kitchen table with Joan, a comfortable menage, leading simple lives without emotional complications.

The following morning I went over to ask Veronica about the room. She was vague on the details and said she would have to check. My impression was she did not much like me, hence her uncertainty. I told her it wasn't urgent and left her gazing out of the window, thoughtfully rubbing her chin with the heel of her hand and arching her beautiful neck. An hour later, it seemed I had misread her because she made a point of coming across to say she had phoned Joan and a room was available, subject to its owner's approval. She looked at me opaquely, and said she hoped I was good at babysitting.

Veronica and Joan introduced me to the room's owner. We all met in the pub at the end of the court, and chatted pleasantly enough. It was arranged that I should see the room. But, before this could happen, a hitch developed. The room's owner dithered about the let because some cousin of hers had appeared from abroad and was thinking of staying. The decision was delayed further when the room's owner put back the date of her departure. In the end, I told Joan to let the matter drop because it was costing too much nervous energy. I decided that my relationship with Veronica, which was failing to make any headway, could just as well be conducted across the court.

During this uncertain period, I started to drive again. After selling my car, I had no intention of owning another, and mostly did not miss one. I had so reduced my requirements that transport was never a consideration. Then Robinson phoned to say that his buyer had lost his licence. A Volvo Estate was going free in exchange for the occasional book-buying jaunt into the countryside with me at the wheel.

The buyer did not look the type to be worried about anything so trivial as a valid driving licence. He wore a tattersall waistcoat and had an army officer background (cashiered). A spivvy moustache and a brown racing trilby completed a dubious, anachronistic look. Robinson assured me he was not nearly as shifty as he looked.

'You the driver?' was his opening line to me. 'Cook's the name. Officer class, Captain Cook to the ORs. Cookie to you, old chum.' My heart sank. 'Have we time for a quick one?'

He played the minor public school, subaltern cad to perfection: the calculated drawl, the hint of a stammer, the insincere flattery, the saloon bar charm. He spoke easily with strangers, was a friend to barmaids. 'She's pretty good crack,' he said out of the corner of his mouth of the one in the local at the end of the court as he watched her pour his Guinness. 'Nothing like the first of the day, is there, darling?' he said, jingling the coins in his pocket. The barmaid giggled. The combination of Cookie fiddling in his pocket and the delivery of the remark combined to make him sound indecently suggestive. Even Joan and Veronica succumbed to his bogus charm, partly because he made no effort to disguise its fraudulence. 'Long as you understand I don't mean a thing I say, we'll get along fine,' he said to me early in our acquaintance.

When times were hard he slept in the Turkish baths at the RAC club. He ran a stable of women, usually married. His buying patterns, and social arrangements, became more complex with the loss of his licence. He spent hours in the shop, using the phone, trying to combine his professional and private itineraries with the help of one of his women, who between them covered much of England. Arrangements were made for collections from stations, and when no one could be found I was requisitioned.

He considered getting a mobile phone, to allow him to work from the pub, the only problem being that no self-respecting person would be seen dead with one. In fact, Cookie profoundly resented change, even in the relaxing of the licensing laws, which he regarded as an indication of the nation's moral decline. He also believed in the citizen's inalienable right to be drunk in charge of a motor car. Cars were invariably called motors. Most of Cookie's slang was self-consciously quaint, as was his racism, a casual old-world xenophobia. He was well aware of the effect he had, and had decided early in life that everything became easier if you invented a stereotype and stuck to it. He had few illusions about his own though he was reticent about why he had been thrown out of the army. The truth was no doubt prosaic. Having

got himself ejected from one of the traditional professional resorts of the not-so-bright, he had tried his hand
in the City, and was caught with his hand in the till,
which resulted in a prison sentence. The form he was
very proud of: 'Banged up in the Scrubs for nine
months.' Cookie played up his gangster connections.
Within five minutes of meeting me he asked if I needed a
gun. 'Pity,' he said when I declined. 'Lovely little shooter
I'm trying to get rid of. Comes with twenty rounds.'

I wondered how on earth he had landed up in second-
hand books, especially as an early remark to me was that
he'd never finished a book in his life. After a spell in Addis
Ababa as a mercenary, he had come back to England and
decided that, for a man of his academic achievement, it
was either books – 'All cash you see' – or the forestry
commission. 'One bloody O Level. Scripture.' Since five
were needed for an army commission, I wondered at the
accuracy of Cookie's biography. Details could elude him.
'Got me there, chummy. Cookie's mind's gone blank.'
He laughed when I pointed out the contradiction in a
story. 'Bugger me, probably made it up.' Despite his
vagueness, he was good with books and had a memory for
them. 'I may be thick, but I'm not half as thick as the rest
of them in this business.'

I came to enjoy his company. He was entirely oblivious to his own failure. 'I say, look at that,' he said,
amused by the five minute sign on the shop door. 'Isn't
that good? Wouldn't mind one of those to hang round
my neck.' Through him I became introduced to a world
of G&Ts, talk of weekend parties, the afternoon racing
form, and hangovers held at bay by the simple expedient
of staying drunk. 'Christ, Cookie nearly overdid it yes-
terday. Steady, steady and down!' This litany would
accompany the first of the day. He had a surprised way
of referring to himself in the third person, as though
talking of someone he wasn't sure if he'd met or not.

Robinson didn't much like Cookie because of a refusal to take himself – and Robinson – seriously. 'That fellow,' he said of Robinson. 'Bit dark, isn't he?' It was true, Robinson had been far more preoccupied since his return.

As for me, Cookie put me down as one of the walking wounded, announcing this as we sped through the Fens in his Volvo. His spit and polished veldschoen were up on the dashboard and he was swigging from a miniature vodka bottle – the glove compartment was full of them – which was then chucked out of the window, accompanied by a loud exhortation to keep Britain tidy. These trips with Cookie bordered on farce. Smut and giggles were a frequent part of his repertoire, filthy limericks trotted out at the slightest excuse. Buying sessions were pushed to the point of collapse.

Out first expedition included a trip to inspect a private library being sold by the widow of a recently dead academic. She lived in dreary isolation in a rectory surrounded by ugly trees full of crows. As we crunched our way over the gravel, Cookie warned me that if he asked for the toilet I was to take over haggling and hold out for the last price he had named.

We were shown around the dead man's library. I watched Cookie carefully: his eyebrows shot up a few times as he inspected a book. The widow brought tea. It was all very civilised: Cookie tried to break the news gently that the library was not worth much. The widow knew that a lot wasn't, but some volumes were rare. Cookie agreed. He reeled off a handful of titles that should do well in auction. 'But the rest, I'm afraid, worth sod all.' The widow's eyebrows shot up. 'Excuse me,' mumbled Cookie, with hasty insincerity, then added that as a favour he'd take away the lot since she wouldn't want them cluttering up the house. He offered a thousand, making it sound as though it were at least twice what any dealer in his right senses would offer. I watched the woman. She looked upset at first, and then alarmed. I turned round to see Cookie, with a terrible leer on his face. He increased his offer to twelve hundred, and asked for the lavatory.

In his absence an awkward silence fell: the gentility of countless teas descended on the room. The mood of drawing-room politeness was suddenly broken by the terrible splashing of Cookie discharging his bladder dead centre into the middle of the bowl; no effort at discretion here, no genteel pissing down the side of the porcelain. This frothy noise was accompanied by a flatly whistled version of 'The Kemptown Races'. The old woman looked as appalled as a duchess caught in a low comedy. I coughed, giggled and repeated Cookie's last offer. She couldn't agree quick enough, anything to be rid of us.

Cookie returned and paid her out of a dirty-looking roll of money, and we had the Volvo loaded in double-quick time with Cookie working at the speed of a Mel Blanc cartoon.

On the road, Cookie downed three miniatures straight off, and indulged in some unlikely remorse at fleecing old ladies. The collection was actually worth, God knows. Cookie had spotted at least two books worth a thousand each. On the way back to London, with dusk falling, we stopped to dump a pile of worthless books in the Bedford Level. 'Bloody sinister,' said Cookie about this desolate spot, and was uncharacteristically silent afterwards.

He made me stop the car on the way back while he produced a ready-prepared syringe and injected himself. 'Ah great stuff,' he sighed and tossed the syringe out of the window. Before I could say anything he sat bolt upright and asked, 'Hear that?'

'What?'

'Music.'

'What? On the radio?'

'No. Not that, the other music.'

Cookie claimed he could hear a soundtrack in his head that orchestrated his actions like a film score.

'Rather disconcerting.' I was sure he was winding me up.

'I'll say. There you are walking down the street minding your own business and suddenly this sinister music starts up.' He put it down to one too many patrols in Belfast.

Cookie played up the business of shooting up, preferably in public and with syringes left on display after. 'Insulin,' he told me when I summoned the nerve to ask him what he was putting into himself, before adding, 'Cookie's diabetic.'

Cookie should not have been drinking at all. Alcohol affected him quite suddenly. After hours of mellow drunkenness he could turn nasty in the space of a drink. 'What the fuck does he think he's staring at?' he would snarl at someone across the bar, minding his own business. He denounced Robinson to his face as 'A fucking poser'. Robinson rocked impassively on his heels and ignored the jibe. Cookie laughed and said, 'Fuck off, cock, is what you're thinking.' Robinson laughed too and obligingly said, 'Fuck off, cock.' Later, when Cookie wasn't looking, I caught Robinson's glare of malevolence.

The question of a room in the Paddington house dragged on. The room's owner was off to India with nothing resolved. The cousin had shoved off and I was back in the running. My acquisition of Cookie's Volvo seemed to tip the balance. A casual offer to drive Joan and Veronica and the children out into the Thames Valley one Sunday afternoon brought home to them the advantages of mobility.

The two women lay on their backs and sunbathed. I was reminded of my wife. Usually I forced myself not to think about her and never to admit I missed her.

After a series of further errands and good deeds for them I was offered the room. I suspected the decision had been theirs all along and was embarrassed that my motives might have been transparent, and for a while after moving in I avoided them.

The room, undecorated in years, was a particularly large, fine one on the ground floor, raised from the road, with a tall bay and wooden shutters. There was a kitchenette area with a primitive cooking arrangement and a tiny gas water heater that lit with the crump of distant shell fire. On the first evening I made an inventory and was pleased with what I saw. A large bed on the floor, stripped floorboards, a single ancient brown leather armchair, and a view through dirty windows on to a plane tree. There were two meters in the room, one for gas, the other for electricity. A wardrobe, a table and a chair with a few shelves above completed the contents.

The building was a Victorian stucco house like thousands of others in London, except larger. Each room contained a lodger. There were communal bathrooms and toilets on the landings. In addition to the rooms on each side of the staircase, there were more in a back extension, which was crowned with a dilapidated and leaking old conservatory that overlooked a dark and grassless little garden with an etiolated chestnut tree. The whole place felt like a boarding house caught in a time warp. Even the rent was still only a few pounds a week.

The sound of a radio, never loud, was often the only sign of life from a room. The lodgers were middle-aged to elderly, shabby middle-class, furtive dropouts and cranks for the most part, unmarried or separated, passed by, urban flotsam. Many went unseen for months on end. One was a theosophist, another gave drawing lessons and a third scratched out a living as a subtitler of foreign films. A contingent of timid and elderly refugees from Nazi Germany made up the rest. They kept entirely to themselves. Veronica's children claimed that one room belonged to an old man who had never been seen, never went out, spoke no English and was provided for by the others leaving trays of food outside his door. The children mocked the guttural accents of the refugees and generally delighted in disrupting the atmosphere of hostile silence that pervaded the house.

On warm evenings I sat in the window, reading and watching the sun slant through the tree, spill on to the table and make its final move across the wall before setting. Once or twice a week I drank with Joan or Veronica in a local pub, usually for no more than an hour or so. Each of us, in our way, had ceased to expect anything. Occasional premonitions of disgrace decided my strategy towards Veronica. I resolved to ask her for nothing, at the same time making myself as helpful as possible, a course of action plausible enough on the surface that nevertheless struck me as slightly creepy.

There were spaghetti dinners upstairs, every fortnight or so, that lacked the painterly composition I'd anticipated. Usually Veronica had one of the children hanging off her while we ate or all three chased noisily through the room instead of being in bed. Her clean and airy apartment stood in contrast to the dinginess of the rest of the house and seemed a world away from my room on the ground floor. It was reached after a journey up four broad flights of stairs through a gloom penetrated by the occasional light bulb that still worked. Veronica's daughter delighted in macabre tales of mutant lodgers with exaggerated eyeballs, grown huge from years of straining at door-cracks.

The only real life in the house was provided by the children. As I sat in my room, I could hear them whooping as they went on the rampage, up and down the stairs and out into the street. It was they who first showed me the empty conservatory, a derelict jerry-built affair, full of cracked old tiles and broken panes. Here they kept their graveyard of mice. The mice were caught in old-fashioned traps, the bodies then placed in household matchboxes, padded with cotton wool, until they started to decompose. Then they were cremated. The children liked the fact that the match that lit the funeral pyre was struck on the side of the coffin itself. They treated me to one of these grisly, formal demonstrations. They also enlisted my confidence by asking if I could get them pure alcohol and a scalpel (for which they would pay) because they felt their experiments lacked sophistication. I watched them carefully reset their mousetraps and replace the matchboxes in their hiding place behind an old disused cast-iron stove. Being allowed to share their ceremony I took to be a form of initiation.

The two boys were innocent brutes, but the girl was strangely feral and sexual, with a candid gaze, and a way of lifting her skirt that suggested she knew exactly what she was about. She was a terrible flirt, and, having plugged so many outlets in my life, I found it difficult not to respond. Eight years old; I was careful we were never alone.

At night I lay on the bed with the lights off and shutters open, trying not to think about her (a variation of the dwarf in the toilet), listening to the noises of the house closing down. The house creaked and groaned as though it had nerves of its own, wound too taut.

I tried to fit in as quietly as possible. We all went out of our way to avoid each other: an encounter by the bathroom or on the stairs provoked the nervous intensity of a duel. Lavatories were watched carefully for signs of occupation. This silent warfare was most evident around the telephone. There was a pay phone outside my room that rarely rang, and when it did went unanswered. Pinned to the walls were little messages in venomous handwriting: Would the person who removed the pencil (for taking messages) please return it, attached back to its proper string. Would tenants please not encourage calls after 10pm. And so on.

'Blimey!' was Cookie's comment on seeing the room when he dropped round drunk and unannounced one evening with a couple of bottles. He was all for dragging Joan and Veronica down to join us. Knowing the racket he would make, I was about to go myself but Cookie insisted. I listened to him banging his way upstairs, whistling 'Kemptown Races', followed by laughter and giggling as they all came down.

It was still light, just, and we sat in the gathering darkness not sure what to say. This was the first time Veronica had been in the room. I wondered if Cookie had come round because he had nowhere to sleep. He stood teetering on a chair to inspect a fungus-like growth that had started to appear high up on one wall soon after my move. I had noticed but ignored, or rather failed to comprehend, it, because there hadn't been any rain for weeks. I watched Veronica and as usual was on the point of saying what never got said: conversations rehearsed and stored, gradually falling into decay. Cookie kept the talk going with an account of slopping out in the Scrubs. This was followed by a surprisingly mellifluous rendition of 'Goodnight Irene'. The others joined in too while I stared at my whisky. Next thing, Cookie was on his feet, still singing, motioning Joan to dance with him. He steered her gracefully around the floor: two silhouettes in the now darkened room, lit by the street-lamp outside and the passing lights of cars. Frozen by Cookie's spontaneity, I sat incapable of joining in, failing to find the courage to ask Veronica to dance. Finally we were coerced into it by Cookie. Her hand was cool, her look defiant and challenging behind a polite smile. I was angered by my indecision, and sensed her anger too.

The party broke up straight after. Cookie stayed and we opened the second bottle and got drunk, Cookie happy to entertain with dirty limericks. I drifted off to sleep and awoke to find the room empty and the door open. Music was coming from somewhere: 'Goodnight Irene' again.

I rolled over and tried to sleep again, but the music nagged me awake. I also realised that Cookie was stumbling around the house pissed and reluctantly got up to find him.

He was on the first floor landing crouched down on all fours with his ear pressed to a little transistor of mine. 'Listen to this,' he hissed and held up the radio which was playing 'Goodnight Irene'. Someone was attacking an electric organ with more enthusiasm than skill.

'Now listen.' He switched off the radio. The music continued in the far distance. Cookie giggled. 'Isn't that clever?'

I was losing patience. 'So? It's just another radio.' Cookie snapped his fingers and before I could stop him he was bounding off downstairs to the basement where I found him standing outside the single bedsit in a state of excitement. 'It's not the bloody radio,' he whispered. 'It's the real thing.'

He waved the radio around with enthusiastic abandon. 'Whoops!' he said as it shot from his hand, hit the floor with a thump and cut out just as the organist completed his finale. Cookie picked up the radio and shook it. 'That's torn it.'

'It's bust, you idiot,' I said, just as the sound came back. A disc jockey was talking now, thanking his contributor for calling in. It was an all-night phone-in programme.

When Cookie banged on the door a suspicious voice answered, wanting to know who was there. Cookie responded with a few bars of 'Goodnight Irene'. The door opened. Cookie pointed to the radio and then gleefully to the very ordinary, fat little man who had answered the door, treating him as though he were Liberace.

We were invited in and welcomed to what he called his studio. The walls were soundproofed with old egg-boxes and the ceiling padded with insulation held up with strips of silver plastic. It was very hot. A portable gas stove burned in the middle of the room. Next to it stood a small electric organ. Cookie was delighted.

The man treated us to a little speech about how he was a regular on the radio show, on account of his dear departed wife. Since her passing he had been unable to sleep and had taken to spending the night in the company of the radio. He'd liked the phone-in because of the communal feeling it gave, though felt it needed brightening up with a little music. After a lot of deliberation, he had phoned in to offer his services and suggested that listeners call in with requests. The slot was very popular, he told us gravely, with letters to prove it. He showed us a couple, addressed to Dear Mr Sparkle (the name under which he played). Cookie studied them with deadpan reverence, and asked who had requested tonight's song.

'Now, there's a funny thing,' said Mr Sparkle. 'Earlier tonight I heard someone singing upstairs, but with the soundproofing down here I was not able to make out what exactly. For hours after the tune was on the tip of my tongue. Then, just before I was due on air, I got it. So I told Geoff – the host of our show that is – I wanted to depart slightly from normal and nominate my own request.'

Cookie said, 'How extraordinary,' and I hoped that was the end of the matter and we could all go to bed. But Mr Sparkle wasn't going to let a real audience escape so easily. 'Allow me,' he said, and with a flourish on the keyboard started playing 'Goodnight Irene' once more, beckoning Cookie to join in. Cookie needed no second invitation. They did 'Goodnight Irene' twice, followed by 'Kemptown Races'. Then, as I was about to suggest we call it a night, Mr Sparkle was on to the phone-in to propose an unprecedented duet. He cupped his hand over the receiver to ask Cookie what name he wished to sing under, nodded approvingly and announced: 'Captain Cook and Mr Sparkle.'

'Haven't enjoyed myself so much in years,' said Cookie with breezy drunkenness as Mr Sparkle hung up and declared that they were on standby. The radio station called back and they were off, with Mr Sparkle getting so carried away with his musical introduction that Cookie missed his cue and almost ruined the show. They were on air for about ten minutes, moving without pause through their practised repertoire and ending with an improvised version of Blake's 'Jerusalem', which Cookie delivered in a clipped military manner that suggested his wind was going. At the end of it, he was bug-eyed and sweating and short of breath. Afterwards, Geoff, the disc jockey, was effusive, no doubt because he had managed to kill ten minutes without having to say anything. Captain Cook and Mr Sparkle were granted an open-ended return invitation.

Cookie faded fast after his exertion, which was just as well, because I had a vision of him wanting to try every other all-night phone-in station in the country and re-peat their triumph. 'Bloody marvellous,' he kept repeating to Mr Sparkle, who was puffed up with delight. 'Same time tomorrow?' We shook hands all round, and I managed to get Cookie upstairs before he collapsed, across my bed, leaving me with the armchair.

Cookie moved in almost without my noticing. At first, it was the occasional night, after one of our drinking sessions, which never reached any formal conclusion and petered out with my dozing off and waking in the morning to find him slumped in the armchair. I didn't mind until he took to ringing the front doorbell at two in the morning, drunkenly waving a bottle of scotch (he always provided) and suggesting a nightcap. The fourth or fifth time this happened I told him to fuck off and left him there.

At four I was woken by a banging on the door of my room. It was Cookie – no surprise – looking sheepish. He had been down in the basement with Mr Sparkle. I pointed to the armchair, went back to bed and switched out the light. He was still clattering around in the dark when I fell asleep.

Mr Sparkle was happy for Cookie's company and their nocturnal meetings became a routine. I found the bald cherubic Mr Sparkle unsettling, but Cookie had the gift of enjoying himself regardless. Although he offered himself as a caricature of a particular class, Cookie was not, unlike me, a snob. He was used too to making his own entertainment. Captain Cook and Mr Sparkle, he explained proudly, were becoming quite an item.

Fed up with being knocked up at all hours, I left the door unlocked. Every third morning or so I would wake to see Cookie stretched out on the floor or in the armchair. Most of the time, his presence did not bother me. He was neat and self-sufficient (army training had seen to that), and wasn't demanding, which fitted in well enough with my leading a life where nothing was expected of me. I had ceased to measure things in terms of human relations. Lists, ladders – of cards and figures –

and small superstitions seemed a more reliable way of steering a course. The tangible quiet of the bookshop, the new video monitor surveying the empty basement, the angle of evening sunlight in my room, seemed more real than the day's encounters: the basement customers were alive on the video screen in a way they were not in reality.

On Saturdays, to give Veronica a break, I packed the children into the Volvo and took them with me to do her week's shopping. We drove out to one of the large supermarket warehouses in the outer suburbs, and while the children ran riot in the aisles, I dutifully filled up a wire trolley, diligently comparing prices for bargains. The children, used to amusing themselves, paid me little attention beyond routine demands for hamburgers and milkshakes. Once, when we returned, Veronica was sitting with a man and I wondered, with a lurch of jealously, if he was the reason our relationship amounted to nothing. It had never occurred to me that there might be someone else.

Downstairs I found Cookie with his feet up watching afternoon racing on a battered old black and white set he had set up in the room. Cookie's comings and goings – an unsettling combination of fecklessness and inevitability – reduced me to feeling like some long-suffering domestic partner, like a wife, in fact. I lost my temper. Cookie looked rattled and uncomprehending in equal measure. Still he didn't move. 'Important race,' he said, not taking his eyes off the screen and swigging from a bottle of stout.

I hauled him up by the lapels and dragged him from the chair, hoping he wasn't trained in self-defence. We lurched towards the door toppled over and ended up on the floor. I lay on my back, panting, thinking how unfit I was. Cookie sat up, shaking his head. He said, sadly, 'Didn't realise you felt like that,' and left.

I found him several hours later in the conservatory listening to the final score on my pocket radio and supervising a mouse cremation. The children were delighted because he was giving their ceremony another dimension: full military honours. Seeing me he snapped to attention and saluted. 'Scoff's on me tonight, sah!' he bawled in his best parade ground manner. What he was proposing, I finally gathered, was to buy me dinner with the fifty pounds he had just won on the horses. The children joined hands and danced in a circle round the flaming matchbox, chanting a chorus of 'Fifty fucking quid I don't believe it!' I apologised for my earlier behaviour. Cookie accepted gracefully. 'Domestic tiff. No harm done. Any time you want to get rid of me, just say. Don't want to be a cuckoo in anyone's nest.' At first I thought he'd said Cookie in the nest.

We ate spaghetti bolognese – ordered by Cookie ('Spag bol, just the thing!') and drank rough house Italian wine in a nearby trattoria. I calculated the bill would come to under fifteen pounds. Part of me was still angry, another part felt sorry for him. He talked about himself all the time, but never in particular and always in a dramatised way. I sensed the present and future scared him, hence his refuge in anachronism and anecdote. I wondered about his women. Cookie was one of those people who always managed to scrounge. Other people's wives and girlfriends were part of the process. They were borrowed too. Even the Volvo, which I had assumed was his, turned out to belong to some acquaintance gone abroad. His whole existence depended on credit of one sort or another (he even tried to get a tab at the pub by the shop).

Cookie's general philosophy was simple, and got simpler in the course of his third bottle of wine. Life divided into those who were good sports and those who weren't. Marriage, on the whole, was not good sport, though plenty of good sports married and it was with them that Cookie formed most of his liaisons. 'Wife at home, bored. Husband knackered by a two-way journey up to the city. Bob's your uncle.'

Ruched curtains, diamond pane leaded windows, Laura Ashley quilts: this genteel territory was Cookie's unlikely domain, a side of him I could not imagine. 'Take them seriously. Take them at face value,' he said of women. 'Discuss frocks and fabrics if that's what they want. Not much of a price to pay, is it?'

He told me my trouble was I was always looking to complicate things. 'Two bits of advice Cookie gives, in case anyone wants to know,' he announced, taking a huge swill of house red. 'Don't shit on your own doorstep and buy your round.'

And look where that's got you, I thought. Instead, I said, 'You have a marvellous way with a cliché.'

Over a fourth bottle of wine (perhaps we would get through the fifty quid on booze alone), Cookie insisted on putting things straight between us. He was at pains to point out that present circumstances were only temporary. His women friends were unavailable because it was the holidays and children were home from boarding school. In the meantime, he was grateful for the space on my floor. 'Besides,' he added, 'I think you need a bit of company.' I admitted I had been feeling under the weather. 'No such thing as bad weather,' Cookie bellowed. 'Only poor kit, ha! ha! ha! Cheers!'

We were the last to leave. The staff sat around bleary-eyed while Cookie drank his way through the restaurant's supply of grappa. The proprietor was trapped between surliness, at being made to stay open, and admiration for Cookie's apparently limitless capacity for his national spirit. By then, I had given up trying to compete and was buzzing with caffeine after sobering up with countless coffees.

'Bloody marvellous children.' Cookie was getting sentimental about Veronica's brats, a feeling I did not share. 'What a bunch.' Cookie liked children because they had none of the hypocrisies of adults. 'If they bloody want to cremate a mouse they go ahead and do it.' I had trouble following his logic, but the vigour of his speech suggested it was all clear enough to him. He stopped in mid-sentence, looking like he had just had a bright idea.

This idea, I found out the following day, involved Cookie looking after Veronica's children for the rest of the holidays during the morning while she went to work. What that effectively meant was Cookie sharing my room on a full-time basis while I still paid the rent. I wondered if he was secretly interested in Veronica, but he seemed more preoccupied by her precocious daughter. 'Ought to be careful flashing it around like that,' he said. I was glad it wasn't just me.

Robinson put in one of his rare appearances at the shop. He came to ask a favour, and to offer some fun. 'Come on, I'll show you.' I flipped the sign over the door and asked where were we going. Robinson smiled.

We walked across to Soho, stopping on the way at a patisserie where Robinson's sweet tooth got the better of him and he bought rich cakes and coffee to take away. He had put on even more weight since I had last seen him. I wondered if he were gorging himself deliberately, making himself bloated and monstrous in preparation for some role as yet undivulged. His hair, still short, was growing out enough to lose its metallic look, and he wore the green leather jacket. He had not washed and reeked of sex. He had a holdall with him and I wondered if he had just returned from a binge in Hamburg.

He took me to a building off Wardour Street. We went upstairs to a cubicle with a Steenbeck editing machine. 'Remember how they work?' asked Robinson. He produced a round silver film can from his bag. Inside was a 35mm four-hundred-foot spool of film, ten minutes in length. I asked Robinson what it was. 'Wait and see,' he said and told me to lace it up.

Robinson laid out the cakes and coffee. Cream from the cake squeezed between his teeth as he took a large bite and grunted for me to begin.

The film was old, made sometime in the forties, and in black and white. The setting was obviously Hollywood, and the event a poolside party featuring film stars from the period. The footage was mute, but well shot. We were in effect watching a weekend home movie shot with the resources of industry technology. Cary Grant drifted through shot. Ingrid Bergman. I turned to Robinson who looked pleased with himself.

At first I thought the film came from the one session, then noticed the same people recurring in different costumes. I found it interesting enough, though not as riveting as Robinson. Perhaps collectors were prepared to pay for a lot of private home movies of the famous. The camera moved indoors. General views established the house, with its mock baronial interior. A shot of the empty grand staircase was held for a long time. As I went to fast forward Robinson leaned across to stop me. A woman's hips swathed in a silk kimono moved into frame. The camera lingered on her figure. It was obvious she wore nothing under the gown. She moved forwards and up the stairs until the shot of her was full length, then turned to look over her shoulder at the camera. It was a well-known face, not as famous as Garbo or Dietrich, but a star nevertheless (her films still played on television). She continued up the stairs letting the kimono slip off her, then turned and showed herself naked to the camera. Her pubic hair was lightened to match her platinum hair. After posing for a moment, she walked slowly and provocatively back down the stairs, sat down on one of the steps, spread her legs, parted her vagina with her finger and began to masturbate. What followed alternated between close-ups of her busy hand and her famous face as she sent herself into ecstasy.

The rest of the reel featured more of her nude, on a balcony and in her pool. There was finally a close-up, lasting several minutes, of her teasing an anonymous penis into erection, and sucking it off: an extremely professional performance in which she never once lost the camera.

'It was her?' I asked when it was over. 'Not a look-alike?' Robinson told me that it was her all right. His theory was that her lover was a Hollywood cameraman who borrowed studio equipment at weekends for their home movies.

A Japanese buyer was interested in the film. The buyer was in London, and the favour Robinson wanted was that I show the film and negotiate a price. Robinson had some reason for not wanting to deal directly. I asked how much he wanted for the film. 'Christ!' was all I could think of saying when he told me. If a deal was struck I was to accept only cash.

I collected the Japanese buyer from the Intercontinental later that afternoon. He disconcerted me on two counts. He was at least seventy, and he brought his wife. She was a homely matron, some forty years younger. I laboured to explain the explicit nature of the material we were about to see. They nodded politely and probably thought I was simple. (I learned later they were among the foremost collectors of film erotica in the world.)

They viewed the film twice, gurgling and chirruping in approval at the erotic content. The fellatio provoked a stream of guttural whispers.

They nodded their delight afterwards, and I bowed in return, wishing Robinson had given more advice on the art of Japanese bargaining. I made a pompous speech about the film's rarity value, ducked naming my price and invited offers. The man bid insultingly low and I countered by doubling Robinson's price, convinced that she, even more than he, was determined to have it. We haggled a long time. Sometimes negotiations broke off and they went into a huddle, muttering furiously.

We settled on a price considerably higher than Robinson's, and I felt pretty good until I saw the size of the bundle of notes they were carrying, at least four times what they were paying, which left me wondering if they'd got off cheap.

I palmed a couple of hundred quid for myself and gave the rest to Robinson, who was waiting in the Blue Posts. He seemed pleased and said there was plenty more to sell. From a brown envelope he had with him, he produced a couple of photographs. They were copies of the official police photos of Marilyn Monroe's corpse and a close-up of the dead James Dean's face, curiously unmarked. He asked me which I wanted. I took the Monroe: a body nude on a bed in an unstarlike room.

'We're losing touch. We should see more of each other,' he said. His mood that evening swung between feverish elation and sentimental depression. He talked about how few people he could trust. I wondered if he were making it up, testing out a new attitude.

We were joined by a young man and woman, both Germans recently arrived from Hamburg who seemed to have an arrangement with Robinson. They wore tatty black leather jackets, had dark hair and pale, smooth skins, and were similar enough in appearance for me to wonder if they were related (shades of the couple in Robinson's apartment). Robinson made offhand introductions. Their names were Stefan and Lotte. They said virtually nothing all evening. At one point Robinson pinched Lotte playfully on the back of the hand, then squeezed harder until she winced. Stefan pretended not to notice. Lotte stared at Robinson with an air of dumb submission, and the atmosphere was charged with sexual tension. 'You should try her, old man,' said Robinson addressing me as though she were not there. 'She likes humiliation. Don't you, dear?' Lotte flushed. I shared her shame and arousal.

The incident, small enough in itself, nevertheless acted like an explosive detonation in my head, and it became impossible to think of Lotte in anything other than fantastic terms of abasement and submission. Until Robinson had brought the matter up, I had not wanted to humiliate anyone sexually. That was his skill: to show you parts you carefully hid from yourself.

Robinson cleaned under his finger nails using the nail of his little finger. He announced it was time to go. I wanted to stay, but he insisted. He cocked his head at Lotte, and said, 'You can see her any time.' Robinson had us in his grip.

Out in the street, the old aluminium container made a reappearance. He slipped a pill into his mouth. It was the first time I had seen him do this for a long while. He wanted to go to another pub. I protested that we could have stayed where we were. 'I want to talk to you,' was all he said.

We walked over to a pub Robinson and I had not been to before, The Crown and Two Chairmen in Dean Street, a large shabby room patronised by a grimy clientele struggling not to fall off the map. Robinson became talkative. He hinted that in some obscure way I fitted into his plans: the dull chronicler, I thought. We sat in an empty corner and he talked with hoarse intimacy about the three things that interested him. 'Power, pain, pleasure, and their exercise. That's all that matters. They're all related. One isn't worth a candle without the others, but you knew that anyway, didn't you?' I expect

I did. He looked at me steadily, and I returned his gaze. 'Good,' he said, suggesting we now had an unspoken pact. I thought of Robinson pinching the back of Lotte's hand, and her simultaneous recoil and look of slack sexual vacancy. I was both stimulated and disturbed to realise how easily, given the chance, I was eager to participate. My mind raced with images of Lotte: trapped and fucked on the back seat of a crashing car; a scalpel blade drawn across the soft white of her breast; her mouth in close-up, like the star in her private movie.

I sensed we were moving into the interior. From the black economy of Robinson's business dealings, he was creating a new realm, a secret market for dark emotions.

We walked across town to a darkened old warehouse in a narrow street in Clerkenwell that looked like it might once have been part of a garment district. Robinson produced a key and showed me in. He guided me through a solid late nineteenth-century industrial space, with four or five floors. Some were knocked through into a single area, others partitioned into corridors and cubicles. About half the building had been modernised. There was a new reception area on the ground floor, with carpeting. Most of the fixtures and fittings had gone. On the first floor there was still a xerox machine and, in one of the small rooms, some basic video-editing equipment. 'Welcome to my factory,' said Robinson.

The building was a victim of recession. The company that had been there had been forced to contract and pull out, but, because of some incomprehensible piece of inefficiency, it was obliged still to pay rent and to provide a caretaker to maintain the building. 'So,' said Robinson, beaming, 'I'm the janitor.'

We continued upstairs and went on to the roof. The dome of St Paul's stood illuminated in front of us. Apart from the occasional rattle of a train going in and out of Farringdon, the district was quiet. The noise of the city lay in the distance beyond. A plane flew overhead, following the course of the river on its descent to the airport, its lights winking. Nobody knows I'm here, I thought, and in two, three hundred years' time tourists will come to the city to sight-see the rotten stumps of what used to be motorway flyover systems. I looked across at Robinson, gripping the rail at the edge of the roof and looking out over the city.

If my curiosity about him was partial and the facts sifted to suit myself, this was because my own introspection was similarly confined. There was much I chose to ignore but, standing there on the roof, surveying the night, I understood why I had waited for Robinson's return. I was the perfect collaborator, an accomplice-in-waiting. I asked him what he wanted.

'Like I said, a factory.'

'Making what?'

'Dreams,' he said with an enigmatic smile.

He took me back to the video room again and asked me if I knew how to work the off-line editing equipment. It wasn't difficult, I told him, just tedious. Again I asked what he had in mind. He shrugged and said he was thinking of transferring the erotic film material he had collected on to tape, and editing it into something that could be sold to private collectors. Video machines were, after all, more common than film projectors.

In the little Steenbeck room off Wardour Street we viewed the bulk of the material Robinson had acquired. At first the footage was innocuous: stars, parties, games of tennis. Some was mildly risqué – stars' private home movies with studio production values and titles like *I Wouldn't Do It in the Lobby,* and *Torture Me With Your Finger.* Both had sound. The novelty of the latter stemmed from one actress, known for her demure screen image, prefacing every noun with the word 'fucking'. There were also early Joan Crawford stag movies, and bondage material featuring a well-known homosexual star who liked being trussed up and having cigarettes stubbed out on him.

I wondered about the risk of blackmail. Robinson thought that star narcissism overrode discretion. One famous Hollywood actor and ex-junkie was even supervising the auction of his own private film library, some of which Robinson had acquired. These films, directed by and starring the actor, were made during long periods of unemployment between comebacks, in exile in Arizona. Now cleaned up and bankable again, the actor's tax problems left him torn between selling off his extensive art collection and the movie library. In the end, he decided on the movies which flattered his reputation as a stud. The performances were as good as anything in his legitimate work.

The films in Robinson's possession featured vaguely bordello settings with lots of straightforward sex with girlfriends and ex-wives, on one notable occasion two ex-wives at once, and various unnatural acts featuring household objects. The tour de force of the collection had the actor standing alone in the desert, naked except for a stetson, deranged with booze and drugs, and masturbating while chanting to the camera, 'Fuck you, Hollywood.'

Robinson's conclusion after watching these films was that we could have made them ourselves. We were sitting in a late-night cafe so Robinson could eat. He complained of always being hungry. He wanted to know if I was bored at the bookshop. 'Not yet,' I answered. I asked what his plans were. He shrugged. 'Maybe we just transfer the stock to the factory and deal from there. Perhaps just sell the lot off to another dealer. Would you like some help from Lotte?' He gave me a disingenuous look.

'Not yet,' I said, imagining watching her in the base-ment on the video monitor.

The next day, while sitting in the shop, I thought I saw my wife walk by outside. I wasn't sure because it was wet and the shop window was blurred with rain. She was holding an umbrella and looked quite changed, her hair much lighter, almost blonde. She was dressed more formally than I remembered. Anyway, my wife was in Boston.

The rest of the afternoon passed slowly. I tried to re-member what she had been like. I told myself the woman in the rain was someone else, told myself too that my wife was now someone else. I walked down to St Martin's Lane and checked the big cafe across the street, and hung around getting wet waiting to see if she emerged from any of the shops.

I wasted half an hour tracing her faculty number in Boston, phoned and got no answer, then remembered it was the vacation. Rain fell heavily for the rest of the afternoon, and by four the lights were on in all the shops in the court. Water seeped under the door and spread in a pool on to the parquet.

A campaign was begun in the house against Cookie and myself. Cookie incurred the tenants' wrath for a number of reasons, and was exactly the focus they needed after years of silent resentment. He was gregarious and in-truded on their jealously guarded privacy. He was noisy, especially at odd hours (whistling in the bathroom at three in the morning). This much we learned from anonymous notes shoved under the door. Some were neatly typed, on an old manual, with pedantic punctua-tion. Others, scrawled in capitals, were more the work of a zealot and accused Cookie of living in sin. We were perplexed by this and didn't see at first that it meant us.

'You are an unnatural who should be cast out of the house,' read one note. 'Nasty business, discrimination,' was Cookie's only offering on the subject, a bit rich coming from him.

Cookie counter-attacked with a plan to invite everyone in the house down for drinks and bring up Mr Sparkle and his organ for the evening. 'Have a bit of a hooley. Get it all out in the open and let them get it off their chests.'

'Not possible,' I said. 'You'll be snubbed. No one will turn up. They've not talked to each other in years.'

'All the more reason,' said Cookie, who'd not been in charge of entertainment in the officers' mess for nothing. He threatened to mix a lethal punch for the occasion.

I refused any involvement beyond putting in an appearance, and even that I wasn't sure about. On the evening of the party, I left Cookie arranging the crisps and nuts, and Mr Sparkle setting up his organ, and went out for cigarettes. A couple of whiskies in the pub delayed my return.

From out in the street the view of my room was not encouraging. It looked like an underpopulated waxworks exhibition of bygone costumes: a taffeta dress here, a velvet jacket there; a handful of guests stuck in frozen poses, none talking. Cookie was like a man demented in the middle of this inactivity. He not so much introduced guests as shunted them together, and frantically topped up drinks. I was about to go back to the pub when he saw me. Had he beckoned me in I would have ignored him. Instead he came outside with jug and paper cups in hand and poured me a drink that was, under the circumstances, difficult to refuse. Like it or not, I had joined the party. Cookie and I stood drinking in the street. 'Have another,' he offered, after I'd taken only a mouthful of innocuous-tasting punch. 'This stuff never fails.'

After two drinks in as many minutes, plus the whiskies, I felt quite lightheaded. 'That's the ticket,' said Cookie. 'Time to let the inmates out of the asylum.' He smiled, tapped his nose conspiratorially, looked at his watch, and gave it another ten minutes before they were all talking gibberish.

Formal introductions were made, instantly forgotten. I chatted with Joan, counted twenty people, then gave up, surprised at so many of us. Veronica stood to one side looking aloof while her children stood whispering in a huddle. Mr Sparkle sat playing his organ, nothing half jolly enough. It sounded like a funeral parlour. 'And what do you do?' I said to one old girl with an excess of face powder and hopeful lipstick. I stared at my shoes – a flash of Robinson doing the same – and wondered if I could crank myself up to some kind of Robinsonian monologue. Before I could, she started talking, rustily at first, until there was no stopping her. I nodded, drank and inspected my cup, which looked emptier than it had a moment ago, then was full again without my noticing, thanks to Cookie's drink patrol. The woman was in full spate, mouth working overtime, me nodding, thinking, Christ, this stuff packs a punch I can't understand a word. She was joined by a friend, a tall, stooped man with the palest skin, and they started talking together and that's when I realised. 'Deutsch! Deutsch!' I shouted excitedly. 'Sprechen Sie Deutsch?' the man asked gravely. 'Nur ein bisschen,' I shouted back cheerfully, exhausting most of my vocabulary in the process. Mr Sparkle launched into a jaunty version of 'A Walk in the Black Forest'.

'I wish she'd stop doing that,' Cookie said, referring to Veronica's daughter who was sucking her thumb and absent-mindedly twisting her frock tighter and tighter, rucking it up until the knickers showed. A fastidious-looking man, one of several velvet jackets in the room,

watched surreptitiously, an empty cigarette holder wag-
gling between his teeth. The girl's brothers helped themselves to drinks when they thought no one was looking.
Thanks to Cookie's punch we all got roaring drunk.
The noise was deafening. Mr Sparkle's playing became
slurred. He beamed at us, his bald pate gleaming. The
children started showing their matchboxes to guests too
sloshed to appreciate what was inside, apart from one
frail old woman. 'Heavens,' she said upon seeing the
mouse, pressed her hand to her breast and tottered backwards into Mr Sparkle's organ at the very moment he
rallied with a musical flourish that propelled her forward
like a clockwork toy into the crowd.

Cookie rushed around topping up paper cups, and
everybody pressed around his jug thinking it innocuous.
The tempo quickened as the drink was guzzled down
and Mr Sparkle responded accordingly with 'Una
Paloma Blanca'. I gave the nymphet daughter a wide
berth, slopped drink down me, realised I'd run out of
cigarettes. The room was starting to turn. I grinned and
raised my cup to Cookie. Someone's dentures went and
we were on our knees scrabbling for them. Applause,
cheering and a sheepish grin from the owner as they
were returned and fixed back in place. Cookie put his
arm round me. I called him a genius. The woman with
the hopeful lipstick made Veronica's daughter repeat in
German, 'The mouse is in his house.' 'Well, this has
broken the ice,' I said to Veronica. Her doubtful look
said she would have preferred it left unbroken. Spoil-
sport, I thought, might have said so too. Off to Joan to
tell her I'd drunk enough to ask her to bed, not the right
thing to say with Veronica in earshot. Cookie warned
me the drink was running out. I looked around the room
and wondered how much more anyone could take.
Everyone was reeling.

Mr Sparkle rounded off the evening with a slow Vien-

nese waltz, requested by one of the refugees. Gradually a
silence fell. A man in a bow-tie and faded corduroy
jacket bowed to the woman with the lipstick. They
danced, jerkily at first, like in a silent movie, then with
accelerating grace. Others joined them, and for a
moment time fell away. No one wanted it to end, this
grave, melancholy procession.

I danced with Veronica, guided by some superior
force. Nobody knew how to break the spell. Mr Sparkle
appeared hypnotised by the effect his music was having.
After so many solitary sessions in his basement, he was
quite overwhelmed by this ghostly kaleidoscope.

We stopped only because we were interrupted by
Robinson turning up with Lotte and Stefan. Mr Sparkle
faltered at the sight of Robinson, gangsterish in his green
leather coat. I was surprised to see him for I had not invited him (Cookie had). His arrival signalled the
beginning of the end of the party.

Realising that the energy was going out of the evening,
everyone made a last effort. Cookie tried to rouse the
room with a singsong: old dears swaying along. It half-
worked. Time on the run, and a grand evening all round,
I told myself. I was aware of Robinson standing to one
side, detached. Drunk or not, the evening had been a
strain on the nerves.

After the singing, people clung on, reluctant to retreat
back into their empty shells. One woman took against
Robinson. It was his leather jacket. Robinson looked
rueful, smiled and clicked his heels. Under his ironic
gaze the guests filed out. Joan and Veronica departed
more sober than the children. Mr Sparkle slumped on his
stool, snoring gently. Robinson lounged around saying
little. I was tongue-tied with Lotte. It was only ten and
felt much later. Cookie suggested we all went round the
corner to the pub for a last drink. 'Not me,' I said, fad-
ing. The others went.

The onslaught of the party left everyone too exhausted to rally. The next day was like nothing had happened, apart from the mess in the room. The house was silent and closed up, and stayed like that. The campaign against Cookie and me ceased. Our real enemies turned out to be Joan and Veronica. 'Why don't you ever say what you think?' Veronica said to me in exasperation.

'Most of the time I don't know what I think.'

I didn't understand what we had done to deserve their animosity. It was one of those rows that never emerged fully into the open. The origins were obscure (to me at least) and it seemed easier to let relations cool. Perhaps that was the problem: our arrangements were at best casual and did not bear scrutiny. Joan and Veronica's downward revision of me had, I suspected, been going on for some weeks. Where I had once seemed plausible I now appeared devious. Unlike Cookie – whom they failed to dislike as much as they felt they ought – I lacked the courage of my convictions. He at least was prepared to dress up his act with a certain charm. He was also at ease with women. I was sure that Veronica had seen my infatuation for what it was.

My patience with Cookie bivouacking in my room wore thin. His constant chipperness drove me mad. Sometimes the sight of him sent bolts of loathing through me. For all his air of social irresponsibility, Cookie was as hard to shake off as a faithful gun-dog (the same brown eyes with a touch of mournfulness). He still assumed his usual officerly manner while undertaking the duties of a batman. The reward for letting him stay was a cooked breakfast every morning, a tidied room and polished shoes, none of which I wanted.

Robinson's trips abroad became less frequent and I spent

more time with him again. I began watching him closely. He was getting ready for some undertaking, stoking himself up for it with enormous greasy meals, chocolate and beer. Gone altogether were the fancy, overpriced restaurants, replaced by cheap cafes serving the starch diet that he now craved to the exclusion of everything else. He relished putting on weight, it seemed. He became erratic in his personal habits, sometimes appearing dishevelled and unwashed for days at a stretch. On other occasions he dressed like the dandy of old.

He began to gather his entourage. Stefan and Lotte were the start of this following. They said less and less, playing their role of fallen angels, pale in black leather. Lotte I pursued, dreaming of experiments in clinical sex with her spreadeagled in a surreal landscape of fractured mirrors that reproduced her carefully displayed genitalia to infinity. She said to me, 'I've heard about you,' and I wondered what stories Robinson had been putting about.

He still humiliated her in little ways. At other times he showed great affection. Both were ways of singling her out. He distinguished her further by persuading her to alter her appearance. Gradually she gave up her jeans and leather jacket for exotic costumes of black velvet and a sinister boa of inky green feathers. Under Robinson's tutelage Lotte was turned into the Ice Queen.

The rest of the group consisted of outcasts of one sort or another, sexual and social, all losers. Without exception they came from a new underclass: victims of recession who in better times might have gone to art college or become musicians. They were young, good-looking and, for all their air of worldliness, ripe for exploitation. From what I understood, Robinson was in the process of buying their affections. He bought them inexpensive meals and let them sleep at the factory, where he paid them to paint rooms. At first I thought they were just the usual crowd of street apaches: runaways, addicts and hustlers who had been picked up at random. Then I saw that each of them had been carefully chosen.

Robinson let me in on the secret of their selection when he took me on a tour one night of the riverside. We crossed over Hungerford Bridge, moving through the cardboard cities of the South Bank and back round to Charing Cross. He was looking for a particular type: losers with nothing to lose. Occasionally he stopped to talk to a figure huddled under a sleeping bag. After each encounter he left a few coins. One face I remembered from that night duly turned up at the factory.

Robinson was careful to set me apart from the rest, both to exclude me and to involve me. We fell into a pattern of regular meetings. Robinson was always there first, sometimes alone, more often with attendants. The boys gave him an air of toughness. We drank in the Angel, the pub where I had first noticed him, or met in one of his cafes. Numbers varied, from around six to a dozen, enough to compete for a place at Robinson's table. The choice of these cafes and their formica-topped tables was a deliberate way of splitting the group, between the elect and the rest. Normally I had to sit with the others because I arrived late, but on occasions Robinson made a point of saving me a place.

Over a period of weeks the group began to take shape. I kept a distance and made little effort to see them as individuals. Barriers of class and culture stood between us and I lacked either the curiosity or confidence to overcome them, unlike Robinson, with his air of intrigue, or Cookie, come to that, with his gregariousness.

Cookie put in an appearance or two, always relegated to the second or third table. He quizzed the taciturn group, forcing it to open up. 'Getting a good screw out of him?' he asked a monosyllabic young Glaswegian, indicating Robinson. I pondered the ambiguity of the question. 'Fair enough,' was the Glaswegian's non-committal reply. I remembered Robinson once saying he was all in favour of the financial transaction.

Robinson was a corrupter, that I knew, but – and here I gave him the benefit of doubt – he was driven enough to achieve a perverse purity. Part of his quest was to seek out the virtue of his own ugliness. Robinson was starting to look barbaric.

The woman who looked like my wife walked past the shop again. She stopped at the window. I was sure it was her, then sure it was not when she looked up and saw me watching. If she was surprised to see me she gave no sign. She went on looking in the window, then came in. The bell rang as she closed the door. I nodded, she said nothing: two strangers, a brief acknowledgement.

She wandered around, went down to the basement. I watched her on the monitor. On the black and white screen she looked more like her old self. She bought a first edition of *The Weather in the Streets*. I wrapped it carefully. Again I couldn't be certain. She was thinner. I looked her in the eye as I handed over the book. She held my gaze, hers betraying no sign of recognition. Perhaps she was ashamed to find me reduced to working in a bookshop. My sitting, her standing, the exchange of money: I couldn't think of a question that didn't sound ridiculous. I wondered if she had set out to ignore me, to humiliate me. Her unspoken message was: whether I was your wife or not, I'm a stranger now.

Robinson began to carry round a tiny video camera, small enough to fit in one hand. He used it unobtrusively, often not bothering to look through the viewfinder, alternating between rapid bursts of taping us drinking in the Angel and long takes in cafes with the camera left on the table to record at random.

One evening he singled me out to sit next to him, and afterwards we went back to the factory where he produced a large box full of video cassettes. 'Take a look at these,' he said, sounding unusually diffident.

The material was the result of all his taping. It was rough, Robinson knew that. What interested him were the people. Who looked best, who had poise, who seemed least aware of the camera. He watched critically, kept asking my opinion.

Lotte had a presence on screen not obvious from just looking at her. The Glaswegian, Iain, had a fearless air about him. Others, striking in the flesh, looked washed out on tape.

Robinson wanted me to transfer all his cassettes to VHS, then select the best bits. 'Good luck,' he said. 'There's miles of it.' There was. Over the next evenings I did as he asked, putting together an hour of material, cutting from face to face, favouring Lotte and Iain, then showed Robinson, who seemed bored. He took the tape away and the next night in a cheap Italian restaurant he was deep in conversation with Lotte and Iain, murmuring, smiling, talking them into his plans. He poured wine until they were all drunk. The little red light on his camera glowed as it filmed us on another table. Then the three of them went off together, their arms around each other.

The following day Robinson gave me more tape. Again it was rough and flatly lit. There were shots of Lotte and Iain sitting around in the factory drinking more wine. Robinson's voice was heard off camera, persuading Iain to remove his shirt and Lotte to take off her top. She did so with no trace of self-consciousness and stood there quite unconcerned by her nudity, gazing at the camera. Robinson filmed them together, necking and drinking on a tatty sofa, gradually removing the rest of their clothes. The sound didn't properly pick up what they were saying and Robinson's instructions were more audible. He deliberately provoked an air of daring, teasing and cajoling them to go further. The wine made them uninhibited and any further tension was dispelled by laughter initiated by Robinson.

Lotte was a star, no doubt about that, putting the more awkward Iain at ease. She appeared to forget about the camera as she delicately stroked him to arousal, whispering in his ear so Robinson could not hear. By the end of the tape, Robinson's camera moves were responding to the action, moving in tight on a kiss, tracing a path over Lotte's white skin: an elementary choreography became apparent. On the soundtrack Robinson's voice urged them on, but Lotte, star in the making, refused.

'She'll do it,' Robinson said to me, sounding like a man trying to convince himself. 'She's told me she will.'

Robinson was serious about porno movies. He had it all figured out. I would edit them and fill him in on what little technical advice he might need to direct: inserts, close-ups, coverage and so forth. I pointed out such films required no great skill beyond making sure the actors performed. I knew from my own days in the porno theatres that the production values and the stories were defiantly shoddy, and not beyond our capabilities. Even so, I thought Robinson ought to find someone with a bit of technical experience to help. 'Stefan,' said Robinson. The surly Stefan was a film student, and ambitious to make his services available.

Robinson's theory was simple. Pornography for a domestic market was a certain money maker. New technology was so cheap and simple that films were now as easy to shoot as home movies. I agreed, but told him there was a long way to go. He needed basic capital and distribution. Robinson looked at me as though I were stupid. 'Why do you think I go to Hamburg all the time?'

He already had his deal. We were to supply a new European satellite porno channel with hard-core material. I asked how he had managed to set himself up since he had not actually directed anything. 'That's why you're here. To tell me what to do.' It was more complicated than that. Robinson had sold himself to Hamburg as a producer. The films would be directed by a man called Ross for whom he could personally vouch. Ross's career in film sounded remarkably like my own, plus a few fabricated directing credits. For a moment I wondered if Robinson meant me to make these films, but of course he didn't.

I was curious too to know how he had stumbled across the satellite operation, let alone landed a contract. The owner of the channel, no less, was the connection and one of Robinson's main buyers, keen to add to his growing library of Hollywood erotica. Robinson raised his glass and toasted our new venture. 'Control the means of production and, who knows?' he murmured. 'It's not like they're asking for anything difficult.'

Robinson's first effort was a disaster. The sound, done by Robinson, was boxy. Stefan's camerawork was more technically accomplished than Robinson's, but lacked touch and distracted the actors. Lotte was self-conscious and bored, and Iain's erection was erratic. What little scenario there was, I could see from the rushes, was still too ambitious, given the inexperience of all involved. Lotte at one point turned to camera and mouthed, 'This is stupid.' She lay on the bed and fondled herself, then noticed Iain outside, playing the window cleaner. 'Do you expect me to cut this?' I asked Robinson. The look he gave me was a mixture of shame and defiance. On the screen Iain and Lotte assumed the missionary position with glazed expressions. She looked irritated as he pumped away on top. Even by the lowest standards to which we aspired, it was no good.

I stood up. 'There's nothing I can do.'

Robinson hung his head. 'It's not worth cutting. Sorry, old man,' I said, enjoying his failure, and went home.

When I got back to Paddington Robinson was ahead of me, waiting on the steps with Lotte. In my room I could see Cookie playing cards with three of the tenants, watched by Veronica's daughter. Given the choice, I'd rather Robinson, I thought, but I remained adamant about not going back.

Lotte was the one who persuaded me, at Robinson's instigation, no doubt. She made a show of taking me off alone for a drink so we could talk. Robinson waited behind.

'Please, do it for me,' she said, offering nothing and suggesting everything. 'Be patient with him.' I thought of Robinson coaching her with these lines as they drove across London. 'He'll learn. He needs you to show him.'

'Tomorrow. Maybe,' I said.

Lotte took my hand. 'Now, please. You've seen how he is.' She leaned forward, her eyes pleading, and played her trump. She was scared that if I didn't go back that night Robinson would beat her up. She was very good.

Robinson and I went through all the material again. It did not look any better. He liked the shot of the window-cleaner's sponge and soapy water obscuring the window, and the rubber blade used to clean the glass. I had no idea what to do.

In desperation I went back to the tape Robinson shot with Lotte and Iain on the sofa. There they had at least reacted to each other. However rough the material, it was spontaneous, and Lotte provided a frisson. We shuffled the tape back and forward until I got the glimmer of an idea. 'Leave this with me,' I said to Robinson.

I assembled through the night. Robinson paced the big room outside, smoking his cheroots. I took footage from both sessions and cut it together, regardless of continuity, taking my cue from the more natural moments, even leaving in Robinson's off-camera instructions from the first shoot. I intercut Lotte and Iain on the sofa with scenes of sex on the bed that got longer and more explicit as they progressed. The material was brutally pulled together until it achieved a hardness not there in the original. The film was full of angry jump cuts. I dropped in random shots of Iain window cleaning, including the close-up Robinson liked, intercut with him with Lotte. As I'd hoped, these added a weird dimension, scrambling the time sequence and making Iain both a participant and voyeur. The device livened up the sex material and even gave meaning to Lotte's look of irritation, which now took on an air of foreboding.

I was proud of salvaging anything from such unpromising material. Robinson gazed at it with an intensity that suggested he was beginning to grasp the medium's possibilities.

He never thanked me as such. However, he made his gratitude plain by making me go through the film over and over for most of the next day, showing him how I had made the cuts. After six hours of this, on top of a night's work with no break, I'd had enough, Robinson's enthusiasm notwithstanding. 'Please,' he begged. 'Just once more.'

'Christ!' I said. 'We're talking about porno. Fuck the cuts! Point the camera and shoot the action. The cuts are only here because you cocked up the action. Sex on a bed and you make it dull.'

He insisted on shaking my hand as I left. Humble Robinson, on the ropes: 'We'll get it right next time.' I sensed there was an unspoken agreement that what I had just cut was only between us.

The rest of the day passed in a blur. I went to the shop, put the sign on closed and fell asleep across the desk.

It was getting dark when I awoke, and raining. I saw the woman who looked like my wife at the window, pearls of rain dripping off the edge of her dark umbrella. I slept again and when I awoke decided it must have been a dream. The streets were dry. When I asked the barman in the pub if it had rained earlier he said he couldn't be sure. I was tired and hungover, having drunk the best part of a bottle of brandy at the factory, altogether wrung out.

I went home and slept into the night, this time to be woken by Cookie setting up a game of bridge with three of the lodgers, including the woman I'd talked to at the party and the man with the cigarette holder, which was still clamped between his teeth. I lay there pretending to sleep, listening to Cookie calling out bids in a parody of strangled Sandhurst. He addressed the woman, who was partnering him, as ma'am, which made her titter. Cookie became Herr Major. The old girl was having the time of her life. She crooned softly to herself, a bit squiffy on Cookie's Polish vodka, but still sharp where the cards were concerned. The last thing I remember hearing was her shouting, 'Polish wodka is best!' and Cookie bellowing back, 'Ma'am, never was a truer word spoken.'

Sometime in the night there was a commotion. I thought it was the game breaking up, but it was merely a pause while Cookie went off to do his duet with Mr Sparkle and the other three switched on my radio to listen.

I woke early to be greeted by the sight of them, still at the table, playing in slow motion now, and shimmering like a mirage in the morning light. The session finally packed in about eight with Cookie rustling up breakfast all round. 'Full house, ma'am?' The smell of bacon filled the room. I got fed up lying there so got up and Cookie barked out a brisk, 'Morning!' as he flipped over the eggs.

When I came back from the bathroom they'd gone. Cookie didn't seem to notice me. He was sitting with a cup of tea and a cigarette. There was a dribble of yolk on his chin. Apropos of nothing he said, forgetting I was there, 'Fuck this for a game of soldiers.'

He caught sight of me, shrugged, and suggested we do a book run soon. Sitting there in shirtsleeves, on his upright chair in the middle of the room, he had the appearance of a condemned man. He looked absolutely shagged out. I saw how enervating this business of a life on the scrounge was.

By the time I left he'd snapped round and was entertaining Veronica's children. One boy sat on his knee and the other two leaned against him while he told them about prison life and his hand worked its way up the girl's leg.

The sentence I heard most often in those days was Robinson's 'I need you to cut some more tape'. He started by refilming the material he had shot so disastrously. Again he expected me to work through the night, cutting.

'I'm tired. Leave it till tomorrow.'

Robinson's aluminium container was produced. 'I'll get a bed made up next to the cutting room. You can crash straight after.'

He proffered one of his pills. I shook my head, but agreed to work after some haggling. I wanted to see the bed made up first. I wanted food brought in. 'Whatever you say, old man,' said Robinson, all kid gloves.

Lotte dozed on the sofa near where they had shot the movie. The bed was dishevelled. Electric cables and video gear lay scattered around. The set looked like the scene of some bizarre technical crime.

Robinson sat with me while I assembled. He seemed unusually nervous and in the end I had to send him out. Later, when I took one of his pills for my concentration, he was lying despondently on the sofa, his head resting in Lotte's lap while she stroked his hair. When I stopped again, an hour later, he had revived and was playing with the camera, taping Lotte who complained she looked too tired to be filmed.

The new material was better. Lots of things were not right, but there was a focus on Lotte's indolent eroticism. I was impressed that Robinson in so short a time was learning to be selective.

Time passed fast. I enjoyed the mechanical, routine nature of the work, pretending to myself that what I was doing was creative and not just production line assembly. I liked working knowing Lotte and Robinson were outside. When I was finally done, I made them wait while I used the toilet. Staring out of the window at the last of the stars, bright in the paling sky, I wondered why everything felt much better, why I should feel I was doing the right thing cutting Robinson's porno pictures. Perhaps this was what I was meant for all along. I laughed. My nerves ought to have been jangled with coffee, alcohol, nicotine and speed, yet I felt calm and relaxed.

I was the first to see the cat, on the stairs on the way back from the toilet. Enormous, the biggest cat I had ever seen. We both jumped, and she shot past with a speed surprising for one so large.

Upstairs, Robinson was filming Lotte again, now making me wait by pretending that my edit wasn't why he had been hanging around all night. I sat down and lit yet another cigarette I didn't want. The cat reappeared. She arched her back at me.

'We've a visitor,' I said. 'And not very friendly.'

Keeping the camera to his eye, Robinson turned to inspect the cat at the far end of the room. The cat stared back, curious. Robinson moved forward cautiously, his free hand held out. He made reassuring noises with his tongue. Slowly the cat's hostility evaporated. Robinson, still filming, crouched down, beckoning. After giving the matter some thought, the cat strolled to meet him, watched by Lotte smiling, arms folded, in the background. I wondered whether this demonstration of trust was for her benefit.

Robinson fetched milk from the fridge, and poured it in a saucer that he put on the cutting-room floor. He told the cat to wait, which she obediently did, as he added a splash of brandy. The cat lapped hungrily under Robinson's approving gaze. Then, watched by the cat, we settled down to look at what I had cut. I sat behind Lotte and Robinson, noting her mixture of fear and wonder as she studied the creature on the screen that was both her and not her. In this electronic zone, thanks to the power of the image, Lotte became properly alive. During the screening the cat jumped up on Robinson's lap. 'Hey, Babette,' he said, and that was how she got her name. She became the symbol of our enterprise with her stealth and air of independence. She became Robinson's mascot.

Robinson and Babette became inseparable. She purred for him, sometimes for Lotte, and ignored the rest of us. She rubbed against Robinson's legs, and was so tolerated that he let her wander on set while filming. Sometimes during editing I cursed the cat: she was in one shot and not the next.

Robinson filmed at a prodigious rate in those first months, alternating between Lotte and Iain and others he tried out. A skinny runaway from Taunton, called Karen, claimed to be eighteen though I doubted it, and thought it nothing to perform sex on camera. Robinson exploited her talent for fellatio. Between shots, she wandered naked around the studio, scrounging cigarettes and gum, and talking in her earnest, dreary way. Although she threw herself around with gusto, she could not act. By then, no one could stand her anyway, and went to great lengths to avoid her incessant monologues.

The end came swiftly when she refused to perform on a polar bearskin rug that Robinson had dug up from somewhere. With a roar of anger, he charged at her. Pursued by him, she ran naked from the room and down the stairs and stood cowering by the front door. He picked her up and bundled her into the street. On his return we all applauded. Robinson stood grinning, swigging from his bottle of brandy, while Babette prowled round his legs. We cheered again – even moody Stefan – when he threw her clothes out of the window and yelled down at her not to come back.

Sometimes during filming, a small crowd of hangers-on gathered and the atmosphere was one of party, with drugs passed round. Besides the usual entourage, there were gate-crashers. Robinson was tolerant of these binges, and used them as a source of talent spotting. They became like unofficial auditions.

More often it was just Robinson and Stefan and Lotte and Iain, working quietly with a camaraderie that extended to me when I put in an appearance. Stefan made it plain that he regarded himself as the only one with any technical skill.

My own position was a strange one. At the time I was the most indispensable to Robinson, yet few of the others knew who I was or what I did. I worked by night and slept by day on the bed Robinson had made up for me, while he continued filming. Usually I came down in the afternoon to watch them work. When the hangers-on were around it was they who regarded me as the intruder.

When there was nothing to do, I sometimes still went to the bookshop though never back to the house. The factory was taking up more and more of my time. Robinson joined me most nights in the cutting room. We could hardly crank out the stuff fast enough for the endless demand for sex on satellite TV. Lotte's films were especially popular. When a station executive – a balding man with a zapata moustache and a well-lubricated cigar – flew over for a meeting we thought this was the start of our success. But he turned out to be nothing more than a bureaucrat with a catalogue of suggestions – troilism, bondage, golden showers – and a list of station requirements that in future had to be adhered to, including one that stated that all partners must be shown to be practising safe sex. Robinson told the executive that we made porno movies not public health films. I was worried about the executive's stipulations but Robinson was unconcerned. Quite the reverse, he took it as a sign that they were taking us seriously.

In fact, there was little promiscuity in the factory. In spite of an air of permissiveness, the reality was an almost monastic one of ritual, order and work. Weekends were abolished. Meals were brought in more and more and eaten at trestle tables permanently set up at one end of the studio. Robinson thought nothing of filming for twelve hours. Insert shots were fussed over endlessly: the angle at which a penis stroked in and out of a vagina – the geometry of eroticism – was scrutinised by Robinson who, for these purposes, adopted the calm bedside manners of a friendly GP, gently rearranging limbs, calculating angles of desire, and propping Lotte with pillows to improve the line of his shot. For distraction, Robinson made Lotte teach him simple German phrases as she lay there patiently. The effect was curiously intimate. Stefan scowled on the edges of this magic inner circle, while Iain, supporting his weight with his arms, tried to maintain his erection until Robinson was ready.

Lotte became immune from all of us except Robinson. Through revealing every crack and contour of her body for the camera, by allowing herself to be so systematically penetrated for public consumption, she both invited and rebuffed curiosity. Whatever ambitions and dreams she was building for herself remained inviolable and unshared. For the moment she was Robinson's creation, but she kept her own counsel. What she said was of no consequence, she understood that, and therefore said little, except to him. They were always whispering together, putting on a public display of affection, Lotte between shots in a flowered kimono that she never bothered to do up. For me, she became more and more like a phantom, a wraith-like presence who haunted the empty studio, coming alive only when I cut her together. I watched her watching herself on the screen and knew she saw something about herself she liked (and had not known was there). Secretly, I told myself, she was mine, to be conjured up in the zone of my electronic equipment. She was the one I loved. Her lack of inhibition I found daunting, her nudity an armour.

The pressure Robinson put himself under was enormous. I've no idea when he slept. He filmed during the day then joined in the long drinking sessions after work, his brandy bottle by his side, and his little video recorder next to it, still taping. He then retired to a desk to one side of the studio to prepare the next day's work, jotting down ideas and little scenarios. This last image is the main memory I have of him from that time: alone, isolated from the rest who carried on drinking while he worked in a pool of light beneath an anglepoise.

After everyone had gone upstairs to sleep (there were rooms with mattresses, primitive dormitories) Robinson was still prowling around, talking to Babette the cat, sitting with Lotte in silent contemplation on the sofa, coming in to watch me cut his work, trying to relax enough to sleep.

'Tomorrow we'll shoot on the roof if it's fine,' he said one night, sensing that everyone was starting to feel cooped up. I was impressed by how attuned he was to the mood of the group, anticipating resentments and rejections before they occurred. But he was looking tired. His skin was pasty and there were circles under his eyes. The only obvious remaining touch of vanity from his previous self was his shirts, which he sent out to be laundered and came back immaculately ironed with sharp creases that survived even the longest day's filming.

He confided to me that he wanted to do something more ambitious, with more of a story. 'Will you give me a hand? You know how these things work.'

I gestured at the monitor, an image frozen at random: Lotte on top, her back arched. 'I'm flat out as it is.'

He returned later with Lotte. Both of them were dressed up for a night out. I said I didn't feel like going. Robinson leant over and switched off the monitor. 'Come on, you deserve a treat.'

Lotte drove us to Park Lane and the Dorchester, where there was an altercation because Robinson and I were not wearing ties. He explained we just wanted a drink. I was tired, I felt dirty and in need of a bath, and was all for going home.

The actor Anthony Quinn was sitting in the foyer. I

expected Robinson to start shouting at the waiter. I also thought they hired out ties, and not doing so in our case was a way of saying they didn't want us. Robinson seemed not at all embarrassed at being refused. He asked to see a manager. Lotte rolled her eyes at me, and Anthony Quinn watched her with interest.

Robinson and the manager disappeared to the reception desk and came back a few minutes later, all smiles.

'Come in,' said Robinson and led us across to the lifts where a bell-boy waited to take us up to a suite of rooms, two bedrooms with bathrooms and a sitting room in between. Room service brought up oysters and champagne. Robinson insisted on opening the bottle himself.

'Cheers,' he said, raising his glass. He made a little speech, toasting first Lotte, calling her his star, then me, his best collaborator. I felt flattered, against my better judgement. We were nothing but a bunch of fourth-rate porno film makers, which, if nothing else, beat the hell out of sitting in meetings with Johnny Repp.

I drank champagne and ate oysters in the bath. Lotte wandered in, idly inspecting the suite's luxury fittings, and didn't give me a glance. She twirled the stem of her glass, and hummed contentedly, getting the measure of this world of super-comfort. I asked her what she thought about during filming.

'Berlin,' she answered.

'Enigmatic Lotte,' I said.

'You,' she said. 'It's always you I think about.'

'Sincere Lotte.'

'Nothing. I think about nothing.'

'Clever Lotte. You'll end up famous.'

'And you, what do you think about when you sit there cutting me together?'

'Seagulls.'

It was her I thought about. Ambitious Lotte, already

putting distance between herself and the rest of us. I told her that we probably understood each other very well. We were only interested in others in that they told us something about ourselves. As passes went, it was pretty oblique.

'Cut, cut, cut!' said Lotte making scissor movements with her fingers. 'Mr Editor and his emotional surgery. Cutting out the bits that make you afraid.' I wanted to tell her she was mine as much as Robinson's, more, because I was the one that put her together.

I stayed in the bath until the water was cold and listened to Robinson and Lotte in bed next door. I sat a long time by the bedroom window, staring at the city, wondering how it would be to feel natural in such opulent surroundings. I thought about Lotte and Robinson with his nails digging into her. The image bobbled about, like a clue that refused to fit. The submissive eagerness I had seen on her face had not been there since. Far more characteristic was that night's stilted exchange, with its cool accuracy and artifice.

I slept badly, my mind racing in and out of ragged dreams, of Lotte spread out on my monitor screen, growing Ernst-like plumage while Babette the cat grew enormous behind me until she filled the room and seagulls beat their wings at the window. Robinson's nails sunk into Lotte's wrist, mine into Robinson's.

Robinson woke me early. By the time I had dressed and joined him, room service had brought breakfast. Lotte was still asleep. Robinson looked quite refreshed. He lifted off the silver warming lids to show me what he had ordered. 'Didn't know what you wanted, old man. So I got the lot.' He seemed in an amiable mood.

The purpose of the jaunt was to pick my brains, which he duly did. He was looking for a proper story, with emotion. 'So far everything we've done is just mechanical.' He wanted betrayal and humiliation. I drew on

hazy memories of Marlene Dietrich in *The Blue Angel.*
Robinson seemed pleased.

We stayed at the hotel until late morning, thrashing
out a basic outline. When we got back to the factory, the
others were annoyed we had gone off. Stefan in particular was spoiling for a fight, which Robinson sidestepped
by ordering everyone up on to the roof. They filmed up
there for the day. Stefan used his technical knowledge to
criticise Robinson's decisions, until Lotte told him to
shut up. At the end of shooting Robinson announced he
was taking everyone off to Hamburg for a holiday. This
turned out not to be possible because no one had pass-
ports, so he took them to Brighton instead.

With them gone, the studio took on an air of interruption, as though everyone had been spirited away in
mid-act. I tried to make friends with Babette who
stalked around, agitated by Robinson's disappearance.
The building, which seemed so innocuous by day and
comfortable with the others there, became disturbing
after dark. I turned my editing table to face the door.

I avoided the place at night, working instead from
early morning through to the late afternoon when I went
to the bookshop for a few hours, then back to Paddington. Cookie had used my absence to move himself in
completely. I was now the one that slept on the floor.
We barely spoke, not after I found him one afternoon
with the girl. I had no proof of anything beyond their
furtive look. But my contempt for him was undermined
by the guilt I felt by association. I knew from my own
thoughts exactly what feelings Cookie harboured for
her.

Robinson came back invigorated, with a script, more
or less as we had discussed, for a thirty-minute film. He
wrote easily and fluently, and apart from rejigging the

dialogue, and suggesting that he cut some because of the inexperience of the actors, I left it as it was.

He shot three more short films in the following week as a way of preparing himself. He grew faster and more confident. The sight of Lotte on screen seemed to free his imagination. She was the heart of his material.

The night before shooting the longer film, Robinson organised his first putsch. Iain found himself dropped, apparently for disloyalty, and in a manoeuvre of some brilliance Stefan was elected to take his place in the part of Lotte's lover. Robinson calculated that the jealous Stefan, as Lotte's former boyfriend, would do anything to keep a hold on her. He also figured that the narcissistic and humourless Stefan would turn out to be a more reliable screen donkey than Iain. As Robinson wanted, the disconsolate Iain became more devoted to him as he sought to reinstate himself.

Stefan pretended to dither when Robinson put his proposal, but anyone could see that he was desperate for Lotte, whatever the humiliation. Robinson made a great show of telling him he would still be in charge of the camera and setting up shots. This misled Stefan into believing that his power was expanding and Robinson was deferring to him.

The question of the other male role in the film remained unresolved until after the start of shooting. Robinson did endless auditions, trying to find someone to play the part of a man obsessed with and humiliated by Lotte's character. Robinson patiently tried to explain what he wanted, without success. He acted out scenes himself and still no one could get it right. Eventually I pointed out to him the obvious. He had to play the part himself. He looked puzzled and shook his head. I showed him part of a test in which he appeared. He was far better than the rest.

Lotte was amused at the idea of Robinson being in

the film. 'Are we going to see your cock, darling?' she drawled. She was starting to get quite affected.

'You won't. Others might,' replied Robinson crisply.

At the start of shooting Stefan threatened to take over the production. Robinson was curiously withdrawn and, as a result, Stefan was insufferable. He made a great show on set of getting off the bed to check his precious camera, an excuse to show off his body, especially his cock, which even Robinson was forced to admit was an asset to the production. He ordered Lotte around, made endless suggestions to Robinson, who was anxious about fulfilling his various roles. For a time Robinson's position seemed precarious, perhaps more than was actually the case. In fact, he had been watching and learning from Stefan, and now knew most of what he needed to know on a technical level to make his own decisions. Although Stefan was still nominally in control of the camera, it was Robinson who operated it and that shifted the balance in his favour. Robinson became the eye. It gave him the extra confidence he needed. It was the start of his period of full control.

When it came to Robinson's turn to shoot his own acting scenes – cunningly delayed until last – he was in command. He hustled the crew along, aggravating Stefan who accused him of devoting too much time to his own performance. He monitored himself on a little playback screen after each take. When I looked at rushes it was evident that Robinson was a better actor than Stefan, perhaps even a better cameraman. He held his own with Lotte too, always managing to make it look as though he wasn't trying.

He and I fought over the ending in which his character was ultimately humiliated after a violent episode with Lotte. I thought he was trying something too ambitious, given the formula. He shot it anyway and asked me to be there. In the morning he drove everyone very hard, picking on Stefan as a way of psyching himself up. By the time they came to do the scene the mood was very tense and Robinson the focus of everyone's aggression.

The scene seemed to work well enough the first few times, but Robinson wouldn't be satisfied. He did it over and over, humiliating Lotte, shouting at her until none of us could tell whether it was acting or for real. I saw why the idea of performance attracted Robinson. To be any good required a kind of fearlessness. (I remembered him goading me to roll a drunk in an alley: 'You'd like to but you daren't'; precisely.) In this case it seemed he had become invaded by the emotion he was trying to convey, until his rage was frightening to watch.

The process went on until Lotte ran from the room in tears, and Robinson declared himself satisfied. I suspected that the endless retakes were about Robinson's performance as a director, imposing his will. I felt certain we would end up using the first attempt, which we did, until Robinson junked the whole sequence, saying I'd been right all along.

I never discovered what he didn't like. There was nothing wrong with the performances. His progress from pathos to violence was altogether convincing and Lotte's fear genuine. As a scene, it was easily the best he had shot. Watching it I wondered if Robinson's films had not been awaiting his arrival in front of the camera.

Robinson shot another ending, an unconvincing promise of consummation between Lotte's and Robinson's characters. Lotte was relieved. She had been left humiliated by Robinson and felt her position had been undermined. Everything she had shot until then had emphasised her own power and command: others, like Stefan and Iain, were subordinate to her, there to service her. Her relationship with Robinson was more complex. The space behind the camera was his, in front of it hers. With Robinson's intrusion into her acting arena the rules altered, and his humiliation of her had repercussions that were more complicated than first appeared. Although the first ending finished in impotence and humiliation for the Robinson character, Robinson's own control over Lotte increased by not succumbing to her sexually on screen, as Stefan and Iain had. What Robinson's performance said in effect to Lotte was: I will not be consumed by you.

Now that Robinson was sure of his authority, his manipulations became less evident. We shot the movies, somebody paid for them and Robinson was careful to look after us. It was a period of surface calm, almost of innocence. Part of the reason for the spell of naïveté under which we all existed, Robinson apart, was because none of us knew what the financial arrangements were, what Robinson's deal was. We were, on one level, doing little more than making home movies for domestic consumption, and because Robinson had selected his group from outsiders and the dispossessed (none knew what a regular job was) he was able to secure everyone's services for bed and board, pocket money and the occasional outing.

He ruled the factory through a combination of ostracism and favouritism. Tears and reconciliations were part of the daily drama that went on behind the scenes. Robinson was careful to build the egos of his actors, even Stefan, treating them as though they were thoroughbreds. They relied on his estimation, which made them vulnerable too. Much of Robinson's power over the group depended on the possible withdrawal of his support.

Word started to spread about Lotte and enquiries began to come through to the factory. She gathered a following and became a minor celebrity, and photographers – usually from foreign journals – started to seek her out. The films too attracted some attention. They were witty and more surreal than other porno movies, their perverse privacy suited the mood of the times. The porno channel became chic in certain circles. Robinson made no great claims for the films. He knew he could do better.

A photo-journalist from Holland who turned up to photograph Lotte also asked to meet the director for a quote and a picture of him with Lotte. Robinson took me to one side and said, 'You talk to him. You be Ross. Why not?'

He treated the incident as a joke, but I wondered if there were not some underlying seriousness.

The journalist was pretentious so I fed him the line that we were doing what Hollywood did not dare. 'Hollywood is death. Count the dead in Hollywood cinema. We hurt nobody. Nobody gets shot in our pictures.' The journalist nodded and scribbled that down. Robinson smirked in the background.

'Next question.' The journalist's lenses flashed in the light. 'Is Ross your real name?'

'Certainly not,' I said. Robinson roared with laughter.

Sometimes Robinson was shooting two or three films at the same time. Their length varied from ten minutes to forty or fifty. One was shot in secret in a room in the Dorchester. Some were started, then abandoned or incorporated into other films. In addition, Robinson kept a diary film of life at the factory, a catalogue of mealtime arguments, biographical sketches, gossip, secrets. Everyone clamoured to be included. It was the most reliable barometer of where you stood, in or out of favour, up or down in Robinson's estimation. Once Lotte answered questions on camera about her earlier relationship with

Stefan. This became a conspiracy between her and Robinson against Stefan. But later, when Lotte had done something to offend Robinson, he taped an interview with Stefan about her. Being in his favour always involved a degree of humiliation.

Robinson had his moments of doubt when he felt he was having to do too much himself because there was no one he could rely on. This was true. Within the space of a few hours he was often required to play a succession of contradictory roles, to cajole, bully, seduce, wheedle, shout. Only at night in the cutting room did he appear to relax. Often he sat by me, scribbling notes for forthcoming projects, looking up from time to time to suggest alternatives to the cuts I was making, drinking – always drinking – and sometimes spiralling off into long monologues that eventually faltered and left him looking blank, wondering what he had been talking about.

Fuelled by his brandy and pills, Robinson pushed himself harder than anybody else. Regardless of how much he drank and the number of pills he took – the familiar surreptitious gesture as he slipped one from the aluminium container – he was able to keep going long after everyone else. But he was starting to need pills to sleep and pills to wake him up. If waking was difficult, sleeping was harder. His brain would not switch off. He felt tired all the time, and confessed that his sex drive was erratic. Lotte was losing interest in him.

I pointed at her on the screen and suggested there was only so much one could take, day after day. We had exhausted the lexicon of basic sexual gestures. Stefan fucks Lotte, so what? Robinson and I were both bored with our material.

He sat on his chair and nodded dumbly, his face slick with sweat. With the weight he was putting on his eyes appeared as hooded as a Tartar's. His breathing was wheezy, and he smelled of brandy. He nodded off for a few moments, his head lolling forwards, then snapping back as he jerked awake. I told him to get some sleep. As he left, I noticed that there was a vent in the back of his trousers where they had been let out: a triangle of material less worn than the corduroy on either side. I asked who had altered them.

He looked a bit sheepish. 'Lotte,' he said. 'The reason she'll go further than the rest of us is because underneath it all she has the mind of a hausfrau.'

I wondered about Lotte's arrangement with Robinson. In conventional terms she was little more than his creature, and her lack of voice appeared to confirm this, plus her willingness to subjugate herself to his direction. At the same time, her indifference and her pliancy to anything Robinson proposed suggested both a calculation and reserve that had scarcely been tapped. Lotte, I was convinced, was perfecting the art of faking before moving on to the next stage, on her own terms.

As far as I know, I was the only witness of Robinson's nocturnal doubts. The days were marked by an increasing carefree extravagance. Both the productions and Robinson's habits rose in cost. The drugs and drink he needed to drive us all on, the meals he paid for and the expensive hotels he used as a way of keeping his entourage docile were subjected to no form of accounting.

The films became more elaborate as Robinson's experience grew. He moved away from the amateurish style of his early efforts with their static photography, flat compositions and poor lighting. He started to move the camera, which required extra equipment. He dressed sets with mirrors, which made shooting more difficult technically. The cast was often left sitting around while the crew went through elaborate rehearsals so the camera did not appear reflected in shot. With these developments came more ambitious lighting patterns, which again added time. The stories, which retained their porno content (Robinson knew on which side his bread was buttered), became more sophisticated. The films were graphic and explicit enough to satisfy their intended audience, but the rickety fantasy elements that I remembered from my days in the porno cinemas were gradually eliminated. The main theme that emerged was of exploitation and, as I cut the films together, I fancied I saw in them an attempt to arrive at an emotional as well as physical nakedness.

Robinson's films, like life behind the camera, became little vignettes on the nature of power and control. At times the two became inseparable. Once, on camera, Lotte made Stefan come too quickly. At first, I assumed this was a way of getting at Robinson, by ruining his shot, but at the end of the take Lotte gave the camera, and therefore Robinson, a look of complicity that said they had combined to make Stefan lose face.

The incident occurred soon after Stefan had confronted Robinson about being paid more. Robinson argued that everything was on deferment until there was money to go round. In the meantime, they were all looked after and fed and paid whenever there were funds. Stefan replied that there would be more than enough if so much weren't being syphoned off by the productions. Robinson shrugged, unconcerned, and told Stefan if he didn't like it he could always leave: there were plenty willing to take his place. Stefan stayed, if only because performing in front of the camera had become a form of narcotic, and for as long as the shot lasted he exercised a control. He demonstrated as much one day by breaking away from the rehearsed pattern. 'Okay, boys,' he said. 'I walk over here, I fuck up your shot. I fuck her this way, I fuck up your shot.' He grabbed Lotte and made to turn her over, but she squirmed free and walked off the set. I watched

Robinson. There was a gleam in his eye. A few days later he had his revenge when Stefan was humiliated on camera.

For the most part, life at the factory appeared to unfold with smoothness. Even the little bubbles of unpredictability – the inevitable clashes of personality – were easy to anticipate. However, there was an alternative scenario I was reluctant to contemplate. Stefan perhaps had a point. Robinson's entourage were scavengers and vagrants, taken from the streets and treated like slaves. His control was a kind of tyranny: everyone was beholden to him. He discouraged any sort of private life outside the group, or secrets within it, except those initiated by himself.

The only privacy I had left was the affair I was conducting with my former wife, which I was careful to keep from Robinson.

It was her, of course. She came again to the bookshop early one evening on one of the few occasions I was there. Neither of us spoke. She spent a long time looking at the books downstairs while I tried to calculate the odds of it being her. Either way, I had no opening line. In the end, she spoke first. The voice was hers. She named a hotel, north of Oxford Street, and a time.

I sat in the lobby watching the revolving door of the entrance. She made me wait twenty minutes, then arrived by the lift. We sat there, two strangers who had once been married. Her conditions were brief. 'You are to make no reference to the past, who you are or anything that has happened.'

She drank her drink and suggested we went upstairs. I followed dumbly, a small-part player in a fantasy of my former wife whose legs I admired (in surprise, not having expected to do so again) as I followed her down the long corridor to her room. We went to bed and there silently revisited places once familiar, grown as remote as a dimly remembered home. After an initial awkwardness, we grew confident, deprived as we were of the uncertainty of discovery.

I puzzled over what it was about Cookie's arrival at the factory that made me uncomfortable, quite apart from my guilty speculations on what he might have done with the girl, and finally decided that, in spite of his perpetual adolescent jokiness, his presence signalled the introduction of adults to our small world. Until then, we had lived in a world of play, of make believe, and of improvisation. Most of the group were very young, many still in their teens, and Robinson's handling of them depended upon an ability to enter into the spirit of their world. He was both the agent of indulgence and its organising force. In spite of shooting porno movies, an innocence prevailed. We were technically innocent too. What we shot had the private intimacy of forbidden games.

I warned Robinson about Cookie, but he only laughed and told me not to worry. Robinson needed Cookie because of his own expanding ambitions. Cookie, who knew a good thing when he saw one, was prepared to play the role of retainer if it involved the slightest chance of advancement. He started by searching out locations for Robinson to use. Robinson liked places where he could film in secret, with as few people knowing as possible. He would tell Cookie that he needed to film in a pub for a day the Thursday following, and Cookie would duly return with one fixed up at almost no cost. How he achieved his deals no one knew.

Soon Cookie was also in control of set decoration and costumes, such costumes as there were. I thought this an unlikely development until I remembered an earlier conversation about the value of letting various women friends chatter on about frocks and fabrics. Robinson tried to combat Cookie's growing influence by treating him as a joke. With his tattersall waistcoat and houndstooth checks, and his parody of an officer accent, Cookie encouraged as much, and responded by treating everyone else with exaggerated good courtesy. He was also the only one who could match Robinson drink for drink and therein lay his power. Because Cookie could go the distance, Robinson tolerated him. Cookie's real talent was for becoming indispensable.

Sometimes Robinson professed to be grateful, describing him as the only one that got things done, apart from myself. As a result, Cookie ended up both managing the productions and running the building, a self-appointed ADC. Robinson's increasingly ambitious productions required greater planning and financial juggling, and since he had no interest in this kind of organisation (being strictly a cash in hand man), he let Cookie take control. He considered such matters beneath him.

On a more insidious level, Cookie made it his business to act as translator of Robinson's whims. Robinson's food obsession grew such that he yearned for a proper kitchen in the factory, a room large enough to accommodate everyone off-duty, with a stove and an enormous fridge full of beer. Cookie organised it without Robinson being aware of what was going on until one night after filming he was led into the transformed space. He expressed his delight, but I sensed his unease at his growing dependency on Cookie, who was becoming the main source of supply on every level. He was the one who said if there was money enough when making a film. He controlled the household purse and hired a cook to fatten up Robinson even more. Most of all, he held the key to Robinson's chemical balance. Robinson's increasingly elaborate cocktail of drugs required efficient administration.

At first it was only the occasional snort of cocaine that was added to the uppers and the sleepers, plus the usual intake of beer and brandy. One could only marvel at Robinson's constitution. Apart from his occasional bouts of late-night blues, marked by their slack unravelling, his mind was concentrated and his lust for filming exceeded even his physical appetites.

The amount which Robinson filmed made it hard for me to get away from the factory to see my wife, tied as I was to the editing desk. I started to see the factory as an asylum: both a refuge, and a place of incarceration.

My wife simply told me when next to meet. Sometimes it was as often as twice a week, more usually every ten days. At first we stayed in her room. The hotel was anonymous enough for us to feel at ease with our charade. Sex was a way of not talking, of not opening up old wounds. These early encounters were essentially hostile collisions between roughly equal forces. If anything, my wife had slightly the upper hand, setting the rules. Also I could not fathom why she had any desire to return to our relationship. I saw desert cities buried in sand, and her, a patient archaeologist sifting through the ruins of our life.

There was the further surprise that we still had things in common. Once we had grown used to not talking about the past, conversation became easy, the mood one of strange familiarity. More than once I was reminded of those children's drawing pads in a cellophane envelope that erase themselves when the tab is pulled.

The horizontal planes of the hotel bed and my editing table became the central surfaces of my life. Infrequent journeys outside the factory saw me hurrying through the streets, looking exposed and vulnerable. Runs to the hotel and – hardly ever now – to the bookshop were the extent of my excursions. Outside the safety of the factory my equilibrium was uncertain. I kept feeling a sense of imminent collision: people became hostile objects, slithering past. Streets looked stretched and distorted, as on a wide lens, the buildings crammed awkwardly to the edges. I wondered if my brain were becoming a camera, the result of too many hours exposed to tape, before realising this disorientation was the result of Robinson's pills. Bursts of speed were essential to keep pace with him, but I had to be careful they didn't clash with the hotel visits. A certain fine-tuning was necessary.

Robinson coped with his own sleeplessness by watching old films ('fillums') on tape in the kitchen when he wasn't with me. He watched anything, recorded at random off the television. He sat at the table, bottles of beer and brandy scattered in a semi-circle in front of him. Sometimes Cookie was there too, his dark guardian angel, playing double-pack patience, a game picked up from me. Robinson's favourite films were old thrillers with sparse stories and labyrinthine emotional worlds. He could remember movies he had seen in the drunken dead of night; I was impressed by his clear recall, given my own faulty memory.

Robinson's entourage became more emotionally tangled as the factory expanded. A rail-thin and severe spinster-ish young woman, clearly devoted to Robinson, started hanging around. She wore a brace on one leg, with a built-up shoe, and walked with a stick. A cell-like little room near my editing space became her sleeping quarters. Soon she was a feature of the place, a sort of governess figure, full of silent reproach, and a source of amusement to Robinson. Irma's influence – her line of infiltration – was the spoken message, relayed via a third party. 'Irma says', 'Irma thinks' came to be among the most frequent remarks in the factory. She sat like a shadow behind Cookie, representing, as he did, a new order. Unlike him, she was a pillar of incorruptibility. Most of her time was spent in secretarial organisation, and attending to Robinson's everyday (legitimate) requirements. What this involved beyond his laundry and taping films no one was quite sure. She soon insinuated herself between Robinson and Lotte, making herself indispensable to both, uniting them in their desire to corrupt her and dividing them with a cold exclusive devotion. Irma was Babette the cat in human form; she and Babette treated each other as invisibles, as if they understood each other perfectly. Irma had green eyes and ginger hair and a skin so pale that the overall effect was quite alien. She made me uncomfortable: I was used to being the watcher in the building. Now I felt her eyes on me, judging. My own reading of her was at odds with everyone else's. They thought of Irma as some sort of mascot, like Babette.

The other notable addition to the factory was Toto the cook, who alternated between a moody butchness and florid displays of camp. His stereotype image was reinforced by bleached hair and white jeans. He was in love with Robinson and desperate to appear in his films. He believed that Robinson should do more to embrace all forms of sexuality. Toto, with his body-building and artifice, represented a mannerism new to the factory, a kind of archness quite at odds with the preoccupations of Robinson's work, so it was to my astonishment that he was given the lead in three films in a row, a trilogy in which Lotte found herself in a lowly supporting part and dressed throughout.

My own relationship with Robinson was still a complicated ritual of parry and thrust, and, as such, basically defensive. But we were both agreed about what we were doing. For all the suburban monotony of our subject matter – porno films for domestic frotteurs – we nevertheless attached a sense of discovery to our enterprise. I fancied that in his work Robinson saw a deliberate opposition to Hollywood. 'I want to see what Mitchum does to Jane Greer after the fade,' he said.

Robinson's scenarios were becoming more baroque. The studio space was turned into a brothel (Cookie's expertise with fabrics giving it a flavour of Middle Eastern fantasy) which was used to create different vignettes within a film. Figures of authority (costumes now organised by Irma) were paraded for the purpose of ridicule. Some of Robinson's work at this time was close to farce.

Again I sensed him flexing his muscles, ready to move on. Part of him was fed up with doing what he called fuck-on-the-sofa flicks. At the same time he was not yet comfortable with the larger crew he needed to realise more ambitious projects. Cookie fussed around on set doing his dressing, rearranging vases, while Robinson waited uncertainly. Irma also took to appearing and advising Robinson about continuity details. (Games of pelmanism in the kitchen after work were always won by her.) Sometimes Robinson complained about how much he wanted to do and how little he had to do it with.

Lotte, who previously used to hang around the set waiting until everyone was ready, and basking in the fact that all the preparation was for her, took to sheltering in my editing room until she was called for. We never became friendly, but we accorded each other the respect of veterans. She told me that relations between her and Robinson were cool. At first he had been considerate or, as Lotte put it, 'He fucked like an animal with the manners of a gentleman.' Now he hardly came to her, and when he did he took her without ceremony. Lotte suspected him of harbouring a perverse desire for Irma and her calliper. A further reason for his resentment was her growing reputation. She showed me a newspaper article with an accompanying picture of her, under the heading 'Lotte Porno Queen'. There was no mention of Robinson.

Robinson's revenge was not to take Lotte to Hamburg. He took Toto instead, to the disgust of Cookie and I who were also invited. Cookie and Robinson spent most of the night before the trip discussing how best to smuggle Robinson's drugs across borders. Robinson, previously so fearless, was developing a paranoid streak. In the end, he phoned Hamburg and placed an order with a contact for what he needed for three days. He remained fretting over the amount needed for the journey. 'What happens if we break down?' We were to drive.

Robinson insisted we all smarten up for the trip. Cookie just about managed to look like something other than a bookmaker. Robinson and I went in the clothes we wore the evening we first met (Irma making last-minute alterations, letting out the trousers to accommodate Robinson's expanded waistline). Toto was made to dye his bleached hair dark. The result was a mangy black and so dead-looking that he resembled an alopecia victim in a fifth-rate wig. German customs waved us through without a second glance.

I drove across the plain of northern Europe, Robinson reflected in the rear-view mirror. Robinson unguarded, staring out of the window, suddenly made vulnerable by the absence of a city around him. It was the first time we had travelled outside London together.

We stopped in a lay-by at a Schnell Imbiss stand and ate fat hotdogs and mayonnaise. Toto took a photograph of Robinson, beer in one hand, wurst in the other, looking misplaced standing next to a cherry tree. 'Silly cunt,' said Cookie with his mouth full, as Toto lined up his shot.

For the rest of the journey it rained. No one talked much. The arc of the windscreens, the spray from the lorries, and the sudden lurches as the Jaguar hit a cross-wind as it moved out of the lee of a truck took up my concentration. Robinson and Toto slept on the back seat. Cookie hummed and made desultory conversation, and I had a premonition that we would all be dead before the end of the year.

I asked Cookie if he ever thought about dying. 'Bollocks to that, old cock!' was all he would say on the matter. He seemed in a good mood, apart from Toto being on the trip. Checking first to see they were both asleep, he asked, 'What does he want to bring him along for? There is a limit.'

The lights of approaching cars splashed across our faces.

Hamburg turned out to be a hotel with a view of a large Mercedes sign, a few car rides, a visit to a house in the suburbs and a trawl of the nightclubs, led by Toto.

The visit to the suburbs involved Cookie and Robinson disappearing for three-quarters of an hour into a comfortable-looking house set in its own grounds while Toto and I sat in the Jaguar in the drive. Toto talked wistfully about the days of risk-free sex, which he was too young to have enjoyed. After a while, I pretended to sleep. It was not that I didn't like him (I didn't particularly), more that I was out of the habit of talking much. Even the perfunctory everyday conversations that had once been inevitable were no longer necessary. If I wanted money I went to a machine: that was about my last connection with the world. Sessions with my wife had reduced talk to a minimum. I'd stopped using the telephone altogether (and what a relief that turned out to be). Editing was a silent process too: it required no speech on my part, although there was a continuous flow of dialogue between myself and the machine and the images.

Robinson and Cookie came out carrying a large suitcase, which they put in the boot and made no reference to.

Robinson indulged Toto by letting him take us on a tour of the clubs of Hamburg. Toto was in his element, Cookie and I uncomfortable, and Robinson curious. For all their flamboyance, these dives turned out to be cautious places.

Not until the end of the second night did Robinson begin to take interest, when Toto took us to a leather club where oiled young men acted out bondage rituals. A man in a hooded leather mask, and draped in chains, shoved a huge black dildo up his anus. ('Like watching shit go backwards,' said Cookie, unimpressed.) A second act involved whipping until blood was drawn. I watched Robinson, watching the stage with intense curiosity, while Toto whispered in his ear.

The climax of the evening was a bare knuckle contest between two men, naked apart from loin cloths. A cheer went up from the crowd when the first cloth came away. Heads craned forward to inspect the man's nakedness. Cookie stared at his drink and said out of the side of his mouth, 'It's like the fucking Roman games.' The mood was pagan. 'A tenner on the schwartzer,' he added.

Once both men were naked they set to in earnest: the audible crack of bone on bone showed there was no faking. Biting, gouging and kicking were all permitted. Until then I had assumed that the fight was choreographed. I watched one of the few women in the club hardly able to contain herself as she leapt from her chair as though propelled by some superior force and drove her hands between her thighs. I wanted to leave. Cookie doubled the bet.

The two fought on until blood flowed freely. Pain was transcended, and both men became aroused. I caught Robinson's beady eye. A chorus of low ecstatic grunts filled the club, building until the crowd was baying in an orgy of excitement, the lust for blood palpable. I watched the woman in the audience, working herself against the back of a chair, her head jerking up and down in vigorous agreement with the violence. She quivered as a left and a right cross finished the fight off: the punched man sat down heavily, as though his seat had been pulled from under him. I came like in a dream. The crowd gave an ecstatic sigh and then started yelling and applauding, and that appeared to be that.

But things had a stage to go. The crowd leaned forward to get a better look. The dazed opponent was lying on the stage barely conscious, his limbs being gently arranged by the victor into a pose of docile submission. then, with the crowd sighing in approval, the winner began gently to lick the blood off the body of his victim.

I told Cookie I'd wait outside.

It was cold on the street after the muck sweat of the club and I drew my coat around me. A roar went up from inside, followed by wild cheers and applause. I had a smoke and decided to give the others five more minutes.

Robinson and Cookie joined me ten minutes later. Toto had stayed on. Robinson was in high spirits. When it became obvious I was not going to ask what had happened, Cookie insisted on filling me in. 'Fucked every which way. To the victor the spoils. That's twenty quid you owe me.' I felt flat and anxious about my response to what I had seen, and slept badly after drinking too much whisky back at the hotel.

On the drive back to London I watched Robinson in the mirror, as he sat calculating in the back of the Jaguar, buried in his thoughts. Toto, his purpose now served, was ignored. Cookie turned the episode of the fight into a joke, finessing the narrative and retelling it with the sort of exaggeration that Robinson once favoured. ('Butch he was and built like a gladiator,' he told Irma, out to shock. 'Should have seen his tool, Irm, could have tied a knot in it. Great flappy feet too. I'm surprised Robinson didn't sign him on the spot. He would have raised Lotte's eyebrows a bit.')

Lotte was resentful because Robinson had not taken her with us. She began acting up on set, picking fights with Robinson, who bided his time until they had a scene together that required him to slap her. They re-hearsed a few times, cheating it. Then, with the camera running, Robinson stepped forward. The slap of his open palm against the side of Lotte's head sounded like a pistol shot. The camera captured the moment in close-up: the blur of Robinson's hand as it whipped across frame; the spurt of blood from Lotte's nose, the roll of her eyes, the high-pitched whine of pain – all made ecstatic by the frame lock on the editing machine. As Lotte reeled, the camera followed, then panned back as she fought for balance and stood looking at Robinson, blood running from her nose and her hand rising to her cheek to feel where he had hit her. Robinson pretended it was an accident. When Lotte walked off the set look-ing dazed, Stefan panned with the camera to show Robinson consoling her: his arm around her, whisper-ing, getting her to nod in agreement.

Lotte bravely agreed to continue filming. Her per-formance thereafter was one of almost magical obedience. The incident reminded me of a pub conversa-tion with Robinson, towards closing time, when he had referred to drink taking people over, 'I like it when you start to see everyone's strings jerk.' I again saw him pinching the back of Lotte's hand, and her submissiveness, both after that and the slap. Perhaps this weakness was something between her and Robinson.

The slap was watched over and over again by Robinson, and by me. The sexual charge of the image was quite clear (and not confused or ambiguous as it had been in Hamburg).

Until that electric moment, which precipitated us forward, Robinson had been content to exercise power by force of personality alone. His energies controlled the daily rhythm of the factory, his insomnia made him the dominant presence in my life. His work I thought of as a form of candid geometry: limbs arranged by him in displays of anatomy. It ought to have been enough, and for a long time we pretended to ourselves that it was, even after the revelation of the slap. However, both of us knew silently that we would have to explore further what had been opened up by those few seconds of tape. I saw a fissure, a crevice large enough to crawl through, and beyond a whole subterranean realm awaiting discovery.

My clandestine affair with my wife became the only norm in my life: the darker everything else, the brighter our time together. Made bold by this, we went out again, and started to move among people. I enjoyed strolling the streets in her company, most of all at dusk, in the rain, under the umbrella she had carried when I first saw her again. I told her I was cutting films (but not what was in them), and the hours were erratic. If she asked me, I would tell her, I decided. I no longer wanted to lie. On the other hand, I didn't feel as though our new relationship was strong enough to stand the truth.

She told me she was thinking of not returning to Boston because an American company in London had offered her a consultancy with better pay than her academic post. We even discussed the possibility of a proper reconciliation. It was, I tried to tell myself, the only thing left I believed in. Or, rather, I saw it as my last chance. If I could rebuild my marriage, I reasoned, I could extricate myself from Robinson. At the same time, I feared that the commitment to Robinson was permanent and my new sincerity towards my wife – this turning over a new leaf – was merely a refinement of old hypocrisies. The slap had become the predominant image in my life, and I was not sure I could resist the lure of it. I clung to the vain hope that if I could keep the two worlds apart – all I had left – then I might, just, be able to pull off an escape.

Every film has two stories: one told in front of the camera and the untold one that occurs behind it. Strange things happen to time while making films, I'd done enough to know that: the curious process of telling a story in the present tense by a working method that constantly disrupts that sequence. Robinson's films were more straightforward than most, at first. The limited sets and scenarios, and the explicit sex, meant filming more or less in order. As he built up a library of insert shots – literally so, as they were close shots of insertions – that could be cut into many of his wide shots, regardless of the film, his plans became more ambitious. He stopped shooting in sequence, and his way of filming became more orthodox. Scenes that occurred at different times in the finished film would be shot next to each other to accommodate the production logistics. Filming, I saw from watching Robinson, was a strange and urgent process to do with catching time. 'Hurry up, we're running out of time,' was a remark often heard on set. This in fact was not strictly true. Robinson filmed all the hours he wanted, and because so little was shot outdoors he was not dependent upon weather.

My own work put me at odds with the daily rhythm of shooting. My assemblies of the material Robinson shot were to do with a different sort of time – organising shots to run in order, footage counters, a constant process of reviewing. I had no command over what Robinson gave me (beyond my occasional suggestion he cover a scene in a certain way) but at my editing table I was the controller of everyone's destiny.

I sneaked out to see my wife who had moved from the hotel to a flat owned by someone we had known during our marriage. The flat, above a shop near Charlotte Street, was empty for three weeks while its owner was on holiday. The night was cold. It had rained and would rain again. It seemed to rain most of the time now. Not that it mattered: weather had ceased to play any part in my life.

I sat a while in Fitzroy Square, a deliberate pause before crossing the boundary into my other life. After days indoors the fresh air made me feel drunk. I thought about the last few months, and realised that if I had to write them up as a script it would begin: INTERIOR NIGHT. My wife was the last contact with the light. Candle light in restaurants, the light beside the bed, the lights of window displays on the wet pavements as we drifted past.

I wondered how many thresholds Robinson and I had crossed since that initial one in Manette Street. 'Ah, fuck your wife,' he'd said soon after. Now, instead of playing truant to avoid my wife, I was cutting time at the factory to be with her. Instead of Robinson being the only ambassador to my secret life, there was her too.

When it began to rain again, I walked on, imagining

her opening the door, the light on her face. These initial welcomes, we both realised, had done much to restore our relationship. It could just as easily have been the other way round – my waiting for her. Anticipation had become a factor again, and our times together had clear, almost formal openings. Both of us seemed to understand this because I neither asked for nor was offered a key. These crossings, from the factory to her door, were like time in suspension: symbolic rather than temporal voyages, towards a refuge of sorts. Too late I see that this was her story too, that I had let myself become distracted, mistaken the many places of refuge I had sought for something more, had avoided confronting the sly dog of my emotions, had taken too many wrong turnings that failed to take into account that our separate interiors were in the end part of the same map, that there was her and there was me, too rarely us. I had framed myself, as though in a portrait, without realising that I was framing myself in another way, to be the fall guy.

I'd known about the target practice in the basement for some time, heard rumours of it from Lotte. Robinson and Cookie were supposed to have brought some hand guns back from Hamburg. I thought it unlikely, given Robinson's paranoia about customs. Lotte said she had seen one of the guns. I decided she was testing me to see how gullible I was. But I did remember Cookie mentioning guns at our very first meeting. I was also sufficiently curious to go to the basement. The door was padlocked.

'What do you get up to down there?' I asked Robinson one night when we were drunk, but he feigned ignorance. In fact he let me in on the secret not long after. A long cutting session had left us tense and exhausted but still wide awake.

The basement was a windowless room about thirty feet long that had been converted into a crude shooting gallery, complete with sandbags and targets that were raised and lowered by pulling a string behind the shooting line. Robinson hinted that Cookie would be jealous of anyone else being down there besides the two of them.

'Whose idea was this?'

'Cookie's. Better than sex, in his opinion. I'm not so sure. Goes well with sex, before and after.'

He showed me how to work the pulley that raised the targets. 'You operate. Pull, count to three, release.'

The targets were life-size military ones, pop art posters with the critical areas zoned in different colours.

Robinson produced a pistol from a chest, some sort of automatic affair that looked familiar from the movies.

'Ready?' he asked, stepping up to the line.

I nodded, pulled the string to raise the targets and flinched in anticipation of the report. The three thin, weedy cracks were not even loud enough to mask the sound of the slug tearing into the target. Robinson walked down the range to inspect his work. 'Not bad,' he grunted. 'Have a go.'

He handed me the pistol. I asked him what it was. It was a fancy replica air pistol, hence the lack of report. I don't know what I had expected: something louder.

I fired off a few rounds, missed twice and clipped the target a third time. Robinson saw my disappointment was less to do with erratic aim than the lack of any kick. He smiled as he took the pistol back, and walked over to return it to the chest.

'Here, try that.' He handed me another gun, different from the first, a chambered pistol. First he attached a silencer to the barrel. 'These things fuck up your aim,' he said, twisting on the fat cylinder. 'On the other hand, they don't wake the neighbours. Aim low and left with this one, it pulls to the right.' I balanced it in my hand, pretending I was familiar with such rituals.

Robinson let me pump a dozen shots at the targets. I snatched at the first couple and they went wild. 'Squeeze,' said Robinson. After six shots I wasn't afraid of the gun. I started to like the way it coughed and shuddered, sending a recoil up the arm and into the shoulder. When I had done the room was heady with the smell of cordite. Three of the shots had drilled the target's head, there were a couple of fatal hits in the heart area, and the rest could be discounted. 'Hey, pistolero,' said Robinson. I was hooked. Point, squeeze and a large hole appears in the object in your sights: it all seemed a wonderfully direct example of cause and effect.

Robinson was aware of my excitement, which was maybe why the next time I was asked down he had arranged for Johnny Repp to be there, just to take the wind out of my sails a bit.

I didn't recognise him straight away. It was his partner I noticed first – the usually absent Dennis – popping away at the targets. Repp was beyond him, knees bent and using the two-handed police academy style. I was pleased to see Cookie hadn't dished out anything heavier than air guns. Repp finished up, blew down the barrel, and twirled the gun round his finger. Dennis smirked. Johnny pretended to be friendly, but was immediately in a bad mood when he found all his shots except one had missed the target.

Why they were there soon became obvious. They wanted to buy into Robinson's set-up. Having failed at everything else, all that was left was porno.

'The word is you haven't got enough money to pay for the paper in your xerox machine,' I told Johnny.

Johnny grinned and Dennis made a hands up gesture.

They were on to the scent of money. Clearly they thought Cookie was a fool, with his sports jacket and Sandhurst vowels. I wondered if he and Robinson knew what they were letting themselves in for.

Later we argued in the kitchen. Cookie and Robinson tried to explain why they wanted Repp and Dennis. The factory needed money. Robinson's whole operation was becoming too expensive and not enough cash was being generated. Repp and Dennis had backers and, in spite of their diminished reputation, they still had enough of a name to raise money. According to Cookie, we had to expand or close down. 'Why can't we go back to doing what we started doing?' I asked, knowing that none of us wanted to.

Once Robinson and I were alone, he tried to reassure me that Repp and Dennis were acting only in an executive capacity and would not be hanging around the factory. I still wasn't convinced. Robinson spoke of his desires, and how he was becoming a victim of his compulsion to record everything. It was his justification. 'I want to see everything. Only when I see it on tape do I believe it. The only time I feel really real is when I catch sight of myself on a monitor screen. Mirrors are no longer enough.'

He asked if I thought what we were doing was in any way important. I shrugged, not wanting to commit myself, and asked the question back. Robinson shrugged, swigged from his bottle, belched and patted his stomach. 'Growing fat is the final luxury,' he said and laughed, before adding that he wasn't sure either, but whatever it was we were doing, he wouldn't want to give it up.

'I like the life we've made for ourselves. The way we've banished the outside world.'

He forced me to admit as much too before going on to tell me that our work was only just beginning. Porno in

movies was a way of crossing more boundaries, and re-
voking taboos. He reminded me of the archway in
Manette Street: the border post at which all obligation
could be left behind. He argued that cinema would progress only when all decency and conventional taste were
swept aside. 'If there's a casting couch then it should be
placed in front of the camera. Movie stars of the future
will be obliged to share every facet of their existence
with their public: MM fucks JFK. Abolition of any privacy should be the price of fame.'

Contrary to my fears, the arrival of Dennis and Johnny
Repp signalled Robinson's greatest period of success.
His devouring appetites – for films, drugs, alcohol and
food – appeared to be all perfectly synchronised. He
continued to shoot at an accelerating rate. His own increasing physical bulk stood in contrast to the grace and
speed with which he worked. His material became liber-
ated from the constraints of its form. It ceased to exploit
and took on instead an air of giving. Even Lotte was
allowed to transcend her passivity. Robinson's films became erotic rather than merely graphic: revelations of
private confidences. His short films, often shot in the
space of an afternoon and on the spur of the moment,
became more abstract, a montage of cut-up anatomies.
He began separating sound and image. One of these
short films won a film festival competition in Holland
and Robinson was invited to collect the prize. He sent
Toto with instructions to pass himself off as the director
of the film.

For a time it seemed as though everything was moving
in harmony. There were gun parties in the basement
with Johnny Repp and Dennis blazing away and declaring themselves content with the material Robinson was
shooting. 'As long as he sticks in the requisite amount of

cock, I don't care what he does,' sniggered Repp. Robinson rode his success well. There are photographs showing the four of them: Robinson, Cookie, Repp and Dennis, all of them with expressions that say they know the going is good. Robinson knew that as long as he was on a roll he was safe from interference. There were even rumours that he might start doing legitimate work, cutting out porno altogether.

Robinson – or Ross, to be exact – achieved a celebrity of sorts. Some smart journalist noticed that the photograph of Ross in the Dutch magazine (which was of me) didn't match pictures of Toto masquerading at the Dutch film festival. Robinson played along with the game by sending Cookie to talk to the next journalist. It was hardly a running story, but it made a couple of Sunday tabloids. One article, run under the heading 'Mystery Mr Porn', printed a photograph of Cookie looking jaunty. Dennis and Repp were nervous of publicity because they feared it would attract a visit from the police to what the papers called Ross's 'East London hideaway'.

Robinson wrote his most ambitious scenario, with the closest yet to a conventional B-picture plot, cribbed from a couple of films seen on television: *The Small World of Sammy Lee* and *The Killing of a Chinese Bookie*. The story featured a small-time pimp with gambling debts that get him into trouble with local criminals. A couple of his prostitutes are put under pressure too. In Robinson's version everyone plays someone off against somebody else. In the end, the women combine forces to double-cross the pimp, who has been cheating on both of them.

Repp and Robinson had their first argument, over the lack of explicit sex in the scenario. Robinson responded by adding an orgy scene (that he had planned all along) featuring the gangsters. Repp's face, as Robinson explained the extent of the orgy, was a picture in itself. On the one hand, Repp could see money being poured down the sink. On the other, there would be many naked women to be ogled from behind the security of his dark glasses. 'How many women, exactly?' he asked as though the question were some mathematical calculation to do with the budget.

Lotte was cast as one of the prostitutes, and Stefan as the pimp. For the other prostitute, Robinson wanted Irma. Repp gagged on his can of lager. 'She's a fucking –' He stopped himself just in time. 'I mean she's got that metal thing on her leg. It's sick.' I thought Robinson mad casting Irma, but said nothing. Robinson gave Repp one of his looks and said he found Irma very erotic. His instinct turned out to be correct. Irma, her confidence boosted by Robinson's faith in her, took to performing with unexpected panache and intensity. Her plain features acquired a radiance on screen and her body turned out to be magnificent and photogenic. 'See?' said Robinson when he showed me the tests he had made with her.

However pleased Robinson was with Irma, he was unhappy with Stefan's performance. 'Here's your chance to act, man. Fucking act!' he screamed, making him do a simple scene over and over. 'Pick up the bottle, drink, walk round the table and deliver your line.'

Lotte came to my editing room that evening and told me how awful the day had been, apart from Irma's first little scene. 'Irma, the new porno queen, who would have thought it?' she said sourly. She also announced that after this film she was going back to Germany where she had been offered a part in a TV series. 'It's shit basically, but it's not this shit.' She made me swear not to tell Robinson. I asked her why she had put up with doing porn. She shrugged. 'Robinson. At the beginning he was very gentle, very persuasive. He made me feel important, no one had done that before. He made me feel the choices were mine. You know how he can talk. He called me his *Maja desnuda*. He put me in the centre of the frame. He said people would look at me and wonder. Also he worried about exploiting me. Maybe he did, worry I mean. Robinson was always very open, at the beginning.'

I asked about the slap. She shrugged again. 'When you were away, I saw I was just his object. It was always his frame, in the end, and me doing what I was told.' She mimicked Robinson on set: '"Hold it there. Yes. That's right." Like a man trying to stop himself from coming.'

She had wanted to leave. He had persuaded her to stay. Lotte thought Robinson's genius was in realising that we were all looking for some sort of family, 'A large family where everyone could laugh and fight and cry and make up. Anyway, where would any of us be without him?'

The early days reminded her of the intense physical curiosity of children, comparing and exploring sexual differences. We agreed it had been fun to begin with, like playing. 'Sometimes now when I see it on the monitor, it looks like a kind of death, everything so pale.' She mimed the panting and the rolling eyes. 'It didn't feel like that. It was not hard.' Lotte on the monitor, Lotte in the flesh, which the more ghostly?

She wandered off and I went to the kitchen for a beer. Robinson was taping Cookie playing patience. Cookie was all mock reserve. 'Get that thing out of my face!' he shouted, loving every minute of it. Fancy card tricks followed. I stood by the fridge with a beer and watched. One of Cookie's insulin syringes lay discarded on the table. The room smelt of beer and cigars. Lotte walked in and ruffled Robinson's hair on her way past.

Robinson was considering Cookie as a replacement for Stefan. Cookie in fact needed little persuasion. 'I'm game for a laugh,' he said. 'Happy to stand in line and

take my turn fucking Lotte if that's what has to be done.'
With that he stood up, dropped his trousers, slapped his
penis on the table, shook ketchup over it, and
announced, 'Which one of you wants first go?' Lotte
laughed but did not look pleased. Robinson laughed,
perhaps at her discomfort. Cookie laughed loudest.

'What do you think?' Robinson asked later, when he
and I were looking at the tape of Cookie. I knew Robinson could make it work. His method was to recognise
and select a particular characteristic and build on that:
Lotte's passivity; Stefan's petulance. Cookie had a seedy
charm and he wasn't shy. In their way, Robinson's films
were always home movies. There was little action or in-
vention beyond a sketchy kind of pretence. Many scenes
repeated moments already witnessed and, as Robinson
saw it, Cookie playing a pimp was merely an extension
of the function he performed at the factory.

The days of shooting became endless. Robinson
would do twenty hours at a stretch, oblivious to everything except the shot plan in his head. Different set-ups,
improvisations, and new scenes tumbled out of him until
Repp and the others became anxious that this new material, for all its spur-of-the-moment excitement, had no
place in the finished film. 'Will it cut? Will it cut?' Repp
and then Dennis kept asking me. Cookie too began to
chip in. 'Seems pretty straightforward to me when you
look at what he's written. What's all the fuss about?
Why doesn't he just shoot what's there?'

Cookie's influence had grown to the point where I
sometimes wondered how much Robinson knew. I suspected dealings behind Robinson's back between
Cookie, Repp and Dennis. I worried too about Robinson's increasing dependence: cocaine, uppers, downers,
spirits, beer. That, and his weight, made his breathing
shallow and audible, like a man trying to catch up with a
wildly looping metabolism.

Robinson seemed to have some private vision of the film that he was unable to communicate. He would fuss over the staging of scenes, shaking his head, then at the last minute change his mind. Some mornings he appeared paralysed with indecision. He began to need vitamin shots to get him started. There were days when there was no filming at all. Then Robinson arrived late on the set, after keeping everyone waiting two or three hours, and mumbled that he had no shots. In the middle of shooting he broke off for two days to make another film with just himself and Irma in his room. This footage I was never allowed to see.

Fourteen days' shooting became like forty, became forty in the end. I began to worry about Robinson's judgement and was by no means certain that the material he was shooting was as good as he thought. It was difficult not to listen to the insidious reason preached by the others. Cookie, Repp and Dennis sat round the kitchen table working out an alternative shooting list which they then tried to present to Robinson, who was skulking in his room. Raised voices were heard, and Robinson's sarcastic laughter as he tore up the list. On these days he never budged. 'We're only trying to help,' was the remark that drove him to the greatest fury.

His moods swung wildly, according to his chemical imbalance, the old detachment almost never there. He became suspicious of everyone in small ways without being able to see the overall picture (he sensed information was being withheld). Lotte bore the brunt of his wrath. He both abused her and stifled her with affection. He screamed at her that she understood nothing, that she was a dumb Hamburg cow who would be nowhere without him. These rants lasted as long as ten minutes sometimes. Her studied indifference drove him to even greater heights of rage.

These outbursts were followed by intense remorse. Regardless of the filming schedule, there were trips on impulse to the Dorchester, long lunches in expensive restaurants, shopping sprees – a £400 overcoat for Lotte, a leather jacket for me. I discreetly questioned Cookie about how much Robinson was costing. Even with the extra money injected by Dennis and Repp, there was a danger of running the whole enterprise into the ground. As for Robinson's personal habit, I estimated between two to three grammes of cocaine a day, plus uppers and downers, at least a bottle of brandy and perhaps a dozen beers. On top of that there was the mounting cost of the film which far exceeded the rudimentary amount given for the basic porno flicks we were supposed to be making.

In the editing room, with just he and I in there, he produced one of the guns from downstairs and stuck it in my face. He accused me of plotting behind his back. I protested. 'Shit on the lot of you!' he screamed before turning the gun aside. He took to producing the gun on set.

The incident drove me further into awkward alliance with Cookie. At first our conversations were carefully restricted to Robinson's welfare. I warned him that if Robinson were careless there could easily be a shooting accident. I felt like a conspirator and wondered at the prophecy in Robinson's accusation.

Cookie and I tried to relieve Robinson of his pistol as he dozed at the kitchen table. He woke up before we could and accused us of scheming against him. We tried to placate him, but he was beside himself, screaming that he should shoot us like dogs. I had been apprehensive enough in the cutting room, though I suspected Robinson was bluffing. Here I was not sure. Of the two of us faced with the prospect of getting shot, Cookie seemed a lot less scared, addressing Robinson with gruff common sense.

Whether by chance or not, the gun went off with a dry cough that I thought was Cookie at first. The bullet took out a chunk of plaster behind his head. Robinson looked at the gun in surprise, then meekly handed it over to Cookie, who was calm if pale. None of us spoke. The television was on and Robinson went back to watching it as though nothing had happened.

Cookie took my confiding in him to mean that we should do something about Robinson.

'You've seen him and what he's capable of,' said Cookie. 'He's spinning out of control.'

I pointed out that Cookie was the one regulating Robinson's drug intake, and therefore held the strings. Cookie pulled a face. 'To an extent.' He suspected Robinson was getting cocaine from other sources beside himself, and pointed out that it was almost impossible to regulate his intake of alcohol. All Cookie could do was to make sure Robinson got up in the morning and went to sleep at night.

I often looked at Robinson, trying to gauge him. His gaze became unreadable, as neutral as that of a camera. His scrutiny suggested worlds where no secrets were left. Everything was under surveillance. Everything was videoed. The camera became the greatest instrument of power.

There was the camera used by the production, which Robinson now forbade anyone else to touch without permission. Even when he was acting in a scene he insisted on switching it on and off himself.

There were the surveillance cameras, recently installed in the building, on approval from a security company.

This deal was fixed up by Cookie as an indulgence to Robinson. Robinson referred to them as his electronic eyes and spent hours sitting in front of a bank of screens set up in my editing room, idly monitoring what all of us did. Watching them, he said, was as calming as gazing at a fish tank. His favourite angle was from the camera on the roof that gave a high view of anyone entering or leaving the building.

Then there was his own personal video camera, the one he made me use in the basement to film the continuation of the work that started with the slapping of Lotte.

I accompanied Robinson into the streets to find his pick-ups for these sessions, standing to one side as he settled terms. He must have explained what they could expect because none complained afterwards. The first one we took back with us, the three of us walking in awkward silence. Later, the arrangement was refined by having the pick-up join us at the factory. Robinson spent this waiting period in a frenzy of nerves, worrying that the person would not show up.

Sometimes he tried it with boys. He preferred them from the tough proletarian milieu, usually seventeen or eighteen. He kept his own clothes on, being embarrassed by his lardy flesh, and gently undressed them. The women he used were usually gentler. All were treated with equal courtesy until frustration bred rage, and then he started to hit them. Occasionally this led to a brief satisfaction, more often to further frustration.

These extracurricular sessions added another twist, the darkest yet, to Robinson's squibby power games. He boasted to me after one of his more successful attempts, 'I play with them. I pleasure them. But I never fuck them.' This was because Robinson, as a result of his drugs and alcohol, was rarely capable of sustaining an erection.

Robinson's chief pleasure came from watching these

basement sessions on tape (sessions, I keep reminding myself, that I agreed to film for him). It required the selective eye of the camera to transform his ponderous beatings. Violence that often looked clumsy and stilted in execution took on a sleazy grace on screen. But, like anything else, these sessions were unpredictable affairs. (It had not occurred to me before that there might be such a thing as a disappointing murder.) I'd previously assumed that, once the final threshold of any taboo had been crossed, complete freedom awaited; that the act of admission into the secret chamber brought its own satisfaction. This of course was not the case. Our work was subject to the same awkwardnesses and embarrassments as any human exchange.

With practice, and because of the uncertainty of relief, the rituals became more elaborate, developed from violence into torture. Robinson's expression as he studied racked bodies was one of almost gentle scientific inquiry. He talked to his victims all the time, never more tenderly than when inflicting damage. His gestures acquired a perverse consideration, his actions not so different from a lover's. Sometimes when I looked at Robinson upstairs, holding court at the kitchen table, pigging out on an endless binge, I saw nothing of the man who took such delicate, even fastidious, care with the administration of pain: the slap, the ejaculation of blood from the nose, the search for the perfect and always elusive frozen frame.

Like astronomers, we became star gazers, creating our own constellations. These stars of our dark movies never saw the result of their work: they were paid off and not asked back. When we succeeded, we were touched with a guiltless wonder. In spite of the elaborations, these sessions retained a core of simplicity – and complicity – lacking in the accelerating confusion of what I came to think of as the upstairs world.

On the screens in the cutting room: images from the separate compartments of our lives. On one, Lotte and Irma in a scene from Robinson's increasingly beleaguered film. On another, private footage of Robinson's victim suspended by the wrists, strung up like a punch bag, with Robinson, his breath wheezy, dealing out pain. When he was pleased with the material he gripped my neck with clumsy affection. On a third screen, a tape of an old movie, recorded off TV. Beyond that the bank of surveillance monitors.

It became harder to get away from the factory to see my wife without alerting anyone to my absence. Our affair was over its first flush, and we were settling down again to an almost suburban interlude. An American colleague renting a house in St John's Wood lent it to her while he was back in the States, a house, I realised, I must have walked past on the night Robinson and I had been reunited, after the Day of Identification. When I went up there I was careful to make sure he didn't have me followed.

I tried too not to reflect on the ironies of my situation. The more monstrous my behaviour at the factory (accomplice before, after and during), the more diligent and caring I became in this elegant house where I walked shoeless across thick pile carpet and stroked the back of my wife's head. We settled into a comfortable domestic routine and rarely went out, except for a drink or two in a nearby pub (not one I had been to with Robinson). Sometimes the sight of her reading, her legs tucked beneath her, moved me near to tears (a passive, domestic image, I noted: my own taste was nothing if not conventional). I felt fortunate that we had found each other again.

With the intensity of work, my grasp of daily narratives became muddled. Events that had actually happened I erased from my memory. Other incidents I suspected of going on, and of perhaps being crucial to an understanding of what really went on at the factory, I refused to confront. Sequences important to development washed through my corrupted memory, their precise order of occurrence no longer clear. Fantasies took their place.

I do remember late one night Robinson in the kitchen with Cookie and Irma when I went to collect a beer. Cookie looked up in surprise, but Robinson didn't, his attention being taken up by Irma. He looked at her with tender affection. The white nape of her neck was exposed as she bent over the table. He leaned over and gave her forearm an encouraging squeeze. Her scalp shone where her recently washed hair was parted. (I wondered how long Robinson had had Irma bending down to him.) Irma snorted the powder and came up blinking. Robinson laughed, Cookie looked shifty.

I invented different scenarios for Robinson, like flickering home movies, random snatches, scratched and out of focus. Robinson the neo-Nazi (the case that he and Cookie brought back from Hamburg had contained Third Reich memorabilia). Robinson the white slaver. I wondered what happened to the street apaches he picked up in the early days, the ones that hung around for a while before disappearing. To what extent I had helped in their selection I was not sure. Robinson taped everyone that entered the building, that was the price of admission, video mug shots that were referred to us for audition purposes. An interesting face might be cast in a small part. At what point I thought these tapes might be some sort of catalogue for prospective purchasers I don't know. Who held them while surgical spirit on cotton wool was smeared on their arm and the needle punched into the flesh, I don't know. How were they transported? In crates marked FRAGILE? Perhaps somewhere in the building was an Orphée-like mirror through which they all passed on their way to the underworld.

I imagined I knew most things that went on in the factory. But I knew very little, stuck as I was in my cupboard most of the time, apart from what I saw on the surveillance screens. It was on one of these screens that I first saw the girl. She was on the stairs, a shadowy figure, aged eleven or twelve and dressed in a sleeveless shift, colour unknown because the monitor was monochrome. I was curious enough to go and find her. I asked how she had got in and she answered she had been here all along. I was confused. I had not seen her before. She wasn't on any of the tapes. The child stared at me dopily. She was pretty in a washed-out sort of way. I wondered if there were parallel films I didn't know about. Maybe Robinson had numerous secret projects besides ours. I told the girl to lift her dress, which she obediently did to reveal her rouged pudendum. I asked her who had brought her to the building but she wouldn't say.

I took her downstairs into the street and told her to go away and say nothing to anyone, and, if she did, something terrible would happen to her. I reasoned that her chances on the street were better than at the factory. Some days later I saw her again, on the monitor that covered the entrance to the factory, hanging about in the street. I told Robinson about her. He denied knowing anything. 'You're starting to imagine things,' he said. We even searched the building once without success, apart from finding evidence of someone sleeping in one of the empty rooms on the top floor.

Robinson was let down more and more by his body. His dependences became both pathetic and monstrous. The torture sessions in the basement were evidence of a terrible despair. Out on the streets with him, I grew anxious in case those we approached had been warned and retaliated by attacking us. How far we had cast ourselves out was apparent from the many rejections we received, the looks of repugnance, saved particularly for me. 'What does he do?' one sharp-eyed woman asked Robinson. 'Hold your hand while you're doing it?' We were trawling among the dregs, among those who regarded what Robinson did to them paltry in comparison to their remuneration.

As the making of the main film dragged on, everyone was convinced it was a failure. Even I was not sure. Only Robinson, with tears in his eyes, believed in its greatness. 'Can't you see?' he pleaded. I shrugged. I was tired enough as it was. Nights were spent after a basement session with Robinson slumped in front of the monitors with their various images from television, surveillance, audition tapes, porno out-takes. He mumbled to Babette the cat, pointing out different pictures to her, speculating what would happen if you cut them all together. Sometimes in the night, Cookie or one of the others would bang on the editing room door, demanding to be let in. Robinson always refused. He had taken to locking us in. We took it in turns to piss out of the window.

One afternoon, after getting up, I found Repp in the cutting room looking at rushes. I asked him how he had got in, but he ignored me. He was on his mobile phone, hunting down Dennis to deliver his usual complaint that Robinson's material looked too much like a movie (which didn't stop everyone, myself included, from thinking it a disaster). Also not to Repp's liking was the film's message, that it was a dog-eat-dog world. Porno films did not need messages, he said. Porno films were low grade, with grimy sheets, penises, vaginas, mouths, rectums, a sofa for a bit of variation, and a rubber plant for decoration. Repp's formula was as basic as they

come: cuntfuck, arsefuck, mouthfuck, not necessarily in
that order. Slow slow quick quick slow. Robinson, he
reasoned, had done it before, why couldn't he this time.
Repp accused Robinson to his face of trying to make the
Citizen Kane of porno movies. 'And we all know how
much of a hit that was when it came out. Nothing. Nada.
Zilch. Fuck the art.'

Repp's anger fuelled Robinson's determination. On
his good days, which were fewer and fewer, Robinson
was amused that Repp saw himself involved in an impossible disaster: a non-commercial porno film.

As the film became more cockeyed and ambitious, so
did the plotting behind the camera. Robinson told me he
planned to get rid of both Cookie and Repp, and start
over again with money from the Middle East, which he
was in the process of gathering. (I doubted it, though his
remark did make me think of crates marked FRAGILE.) I
imagined a parallel plot to Cookie, Repp and Dennis
that involved, without Robinson's knowledge, the
shooting of kiddie porn in the empty attic of the next-
door building: hence the girl on the stairs.

Robinson's exasperation with Repp reached a climax
on the set. Repp was agitated because there had been no
filming for three days. When on the fourth day Robinson finally turned up, he had no shots in mind. Repp
started telling Robinson what to do. His glasses had
darkened under the lights and Robinson leaned forward
to say he wouldn't talk to a man whose eyes he couldn't
see. He gently removed Repp's glasses, folded them and
snapped them in two. Repp's eyes popped with surprise.
Then Robinson butted him. Repp yelped his way off the
set, hands clutched to his nose.

After that, he stayed away, but I fancied we had not
heard the last of him, and that Robinson had made a
powerful enemy.

Robinson turned to focus his aggression on Cookie.

He felt degraded by his dependency upon him for his drugs, and now called him 'Nurse' to his face. He blamed 'Nurse' for introducing what he called the Repp virus into the factory. 'About time we got rid of you, Nurse,' Robinson announced at meals.

With no end of shooting in sight, everyone was strung out with exhaustion. After filming hours at a stretch, no one was capable of relaxing until protracted and indiscriminate drinking had rendered them senseless. Days became one long hangover for cast and crew.

As the filming deteriorated, Robinson too started to lose confidence and to think the film was a mess. His nights were spent hiding from the uncertainty of his days. When we were in the cutting room Robinson ignored the material I was working on and concentrated instead on an idea he had of making a map of images from all the material we had assembled: ours, other people's, television, films, news bulletins. This film would suggest all nature of images, it would be both a map and a cathedral. He started trying out different little cuts but I didn't think he was serious. One cut was from the snow shaker breaking at the start of *Citizen Kane* to amateur footage shot in the 1930s of an anonymous woman in a window of an English seaside resort, and her view down on to the esplanade on a rainy summer afternoon. I found the cut obscurely moving and puzzled as to why. Perhaps it was the breadth suggested by it. Robinson seemed calm and preoccupied fiddling around with his bits of found footage so I encouraged him to get on with it. For perhaps a week or so we stayed off the streets.

On the night of hitting Johnny Repp he lapsed. He said he was too busy to go out himself but felt the need to tape some material later in the basement, and asked me to find someone off the streets. I tried to make excuses, but he pleaded, close to tears.

I went, and didn't bother. In my grand, skewed estimate of myself, I was prepared to go so far but I wasn't pimping for Robinson. I wandered around the damp streets for a while, then went back and lied. When nobody showed up he was disappointed rather than angry. He couldn't prove it, of course, so I stood my ground.

Robinson's suffering was obvious. He was breathing poorly. His different addictions jostled with each other, short-circuiting his body system: I waited for him to start crackling and fusing like a failing circuit. I told him he ought to be careful. One of these days he would get the dose wrong. Robinson gave me a look of strange tenderness, like an adult to a child he knows has lied. 'Just help me through the next few days,' he said with great weariness. I agreed to search the streets with him.

A whole shanty town had sprung up in the last few weeks in an abandoned development site, quite close to the factory. Some of the inhabitants of this cardboard city were little more than children, who fled from our approach. Robinson negotiated with a skinny woman, who agreed to go with him, and we trooped off watched by suspicious eyes. A few jeers followed us.

With the skinny woman he went too far. He frightened her and when she started yelling he felt obliged to shut her up. He gagged her with his hand and when she bit that and began screaming he grabbed her arm, threw her against the wall, slapped her face with a rising backhand that rattled her teeth and chopped her neck with the heel of his hand as she bent double with the pain. She fell to the ground and I thought he had killed her. I dragged him away and for a moment feared he would attack me. This was the first time he had lost control so completely. The woman stirred and shifted. Robinson's libido unexpectedly returned. He wanted to fuck her. No, I told him, absolutely not. Robinson shrugged helplessly and rummaged inside his trousers. Then leaning one hand against the wall, and with the expression of a man drowning in sorrow, he masturbated until he came, making sure I was taping him.

Afterwards, he made me drive the still unconscious woman away and dump her with some money in her pocket. She came round as I pulled her from the car and started cursing me. I'd not really thought of the others as people, more like flesh to be sculpted, but this one really got under my skin. I threw some more money at her and fled.

I found Robinson at the kitchen table with a tumbler of brandy in front of him. He held his head in his hands. 'None of this would happen if I could sleep.'

Cookie interrupted us. 'Ah fuck off,' said Robinson as soon as he put his head round the door. 'We're having a private conversation.'

Cookie ignored him, fetched a beer from the fridge, and sat down at the table, and there we sat in silence as the dawn came up and Robinson's head fell forward on to his chest and he started snoring. Cookie looked at his watch and said, 'Shooting in three hours.' He gave me a knowing look, to say he was quite aware of what Robinson and I got up to.

How Robinson was ready in time for that day's filming, I have no idea. When I saw him, at around noon, he looked beyond exhaustion. He massaged a tender spot under his heart. Yet in spite of his appearance he seemed cheerful and was caught up in the shooting, scribbling out his plan for the afternoon.

That night I got Robinson to bed at something approaching a reasonable hour, which let me slip off to St John's Wood. The telephone there almost never rang, and when it did it was for the absent owner. Even so I worried that it might be Robinson, tracking me down. My wife invariably said, 'I doubt if it's for us. Don't bother.' 'Well,' I'd reply, getting up, 'I can take a message.' I found myself taking a breath before picking up the receiver, half-expecting to hear his familiar voice. I was under no illusions that my wife would denounce me if she ever did find out what I was up to.

I wondered if Robinson's insomnia was catching as I lay awake in the dark listening to the rain. When I fell asleep it was to dream of an enormous tape unspooling and flooding the room.

It was still raining when I arrived back at the factory.

Robinson had me out prowling the streets with him again. On the edge of the cardboard city we were set upon. I had pleaded with him not to look for pick-ups there because I was afraid of exactly that. I'd urged him to go down to the river, but he was in too much of a hurry. Four tough-looking youths cornered us. Robinson looked calm. My own reaction was the usual middle-class one of protesting that this was not fair. But fear of losing face frightened me even more. I prayed for a miracle.

Robinson slipped his hand in his pocket. For a second I thought he was going to produce his aluminium container, but this particular sneaky little conjuring trick ended with the gun in his fist. The sight of its snout aimed at them checked the youths. After a quick conference, they decided the gun wasn't real and closed in, less certainly. The silenced gun gave its little cough and mud splattered over the shoes of the ringleader.

Robinson made the most of the lad's humiliation. From a confident young tough he was transformed into a gawky youth with an overlarge adam's apple. When Robinson was satisfied, he clubbed the boy across the head with the butt of his pistol and left him lying there bleeding. The others ran.

Far from having had enough, Robinson insisted on

going deeper into the cardboard city. I dared not leave him. At the same time, I felt even less safe at the prospect of a trawl through this shanty town, gun or no gun. Robinson turned on me angrily and told me to pull myself together. What annoyed me most was that he had seen my fear.

It rained again as we picked our way through the sodden boxes. Pasty faces shrank back into the shadows as we passed. Ruining my shoes made me even more peevish. He finally found a boy to go with us.

At first Robinson seemed in an almost gentle mood, working with a quiet ecstasy, bandaging the boy's hands, as though they were wounded, then tying his arms and legs to a chair. He gagged the boy, wrapped a silk scarf around his neck and began to pull. Robinson looked across at me and told me to tape in close-up. The boy's face was suffused with blood, his eyes popping. I told him to stop, he'd gone mad. Robinson was furious, and shouted at me that he knew what he was doing. 'You stupid fool,' he yelled, spittle flying. 'Can't you see, he likes it.'

I took my eye away from the viewfinder. The boy had an erection. For Robinson, though, the moment was lost with my interruption. He hastily untied the boy, who stood there too scared to leave until Robinson roared at him to get out.

On set the next day Robinson and Lotte had a row so huge that news of it reached me as it was going on. I arrived to find Lotte threatening to kill herself. Robinson, on his knees, pleaded with her, told her she was the only one he had ever loved.

She accused him of being incapable of caring for her, or anyone, until he had destroyed them. Robinson clutched his head and accused everyone in the room of conspiring against him. 'You're killing me, all of you!' he shouted, before charging us with being too cowardly to take him on individually. He tugged his shirt open, revealing his white and hairless chest. 'What do you want of me? Which bit do you want?' Robinson bared his arm. 'This bit?'

No one would challenge him. We were too weak, weak in vision. As embarrassed as we were by this display, we were even more scared of the prospect of the whole party coming to an end.

Robinson's performance ended with him urinating on the floor, saying, 'I piss on you all from a great height.'

'Et tu, Brute,' he said quietly to me, on his way out of the room. I looked him in the eye. It was deliberate and calculating. His melodramatic performance had been entirely for effect. Lotte, on the other hand, was still shaking.

After lunch there were flowers for Lotte, an enormous spray of them from Robinson. There were kisses and tears as they made up. The mood was cheerful again. 'Back to work everyone,' shouted Robinson, who seemed rejuvenated.

I refused to connect up the increasing violence, to see it as part of an accelerating pattern. Instead I told myself the usual daily rhythm would reassert itself. Anyway, soon it would be over. After the shooting Lotte was leaving, and I would slip away too.

As filming ground on, Robinson appeared more and more distracted. He sat at night in front of an editing screen playing with all the footage he had collected. He cut together a montage of people dying – actors dying in movies, people dying in news footage, old newsreels. He replayed it endlessly, sometimes stopping the tape to look at a cut again. Then he slapped his hand on the table as though the accident of the cut had revealed some astonishing truth. I saw only a hopeless scrapbook of deathly images, the work of a man at the end of his tether.

This growing obsession with death led him to suspend shooting yet again while he worked on a new story. As far as I could see, the sheer impossibility of it was its only attraction. Dennis read it and shook his head.

The story had developed out of two photographs: one of Warner Bros studios in the 1940s, the other of Auschwitz. Robinson had been struck by the similarity. He called his outline *Hollywood/Treblinka* and in it traced the different fates of a European Jewish family in the 1940s, some of whom are interned while others escape to California and eke out a miserable living on the fringes of the movie business as extras. Robinson found in both systems ghostly echoes of the other: one being the perfect, negative assembly line conditioned to manufacture death; the other an apparatus whose enormous machinery was dedicated to producing phantoms. Robinson called this project the ultimate porno movie. 'You're sick,' said Dennis. 'You know that? Really, really sick.'

Robinson lost himself in the belief that he would make this new film, regardless of cost. Like a man with a last chance, Robinson seemed in desperate search for one idea that would make sense of it all. As gently as I could I tried to steer him back to the film we were supposed to be cutting, which in truth seemed just a part of this greater senselessness.

Robinson's earlier conviction had ebbed away to be replaced by a complete loathing for the film he was making. He started to blame its failure on others, Stefan in particular for not coming up to scratch on the first day. Irma, he now decided, was completely unerotic and he had been mad to cast her. He grew bored and disenchanted. He encouraged Lotte to yawn during one sex scene. The fact that Cookie acted passably well drove him into towering rages that usually ended up falling on me in the middle of the night in the cutting room.

Everything was out of whack. We all felt it. It was like finding we were running on the spot after all, and not moving forward as we'd thought. Any sense of narrative that had guided everyone at the beginning had long vanished. The project drifted, day after day of mechanical assembly, on the days that shooting began at all. Spurts of hostility erupted on the set to interrupt the mood of sullen exhaustion. Then even they subsided and bickering was all anyone could rise to. I was surprised we carried on, that there was not a refusal to work, except that in itself would have required an energy no one could summon.

The mood of the film was reflected in the weather, which was hot, grey and oppressive, with sudden bursts of rain that brought no relief. The heat did not help. On the set the predominant smells were of sweat and sex and the dry burning of an overloaded electrical circuit. The worse it got, the more we looked to Robinson for the miracle that he could or would not provide.

He shot the orgy scene and took days over it. Even Repp made a reappearance for that. He and Robinson studiously ignored each other. The contrast between the skittish behaviour of the extras and the battle-fatigued members of the factory led to a further souring of the atmosphere. Past and future had fallen away entirely. No one talked of the film actually ending. We were stuck in a remorseless, grinding present that had no end.

While Robinson loitered over his orgy scene I slipped away to St John's Wood for a brief respite that made the return to the factory seem all the more pointless.

As the last couple of days of filming approached it became apparent the film would not be finished. Robinson was refusing to make up his mind about the ending. The original story was not, on the evidence of what I'd seen, what had been shot. (The rushes made no sense and

Repp had every right to be worried.) Parts of the original had been covered, others junked and replaced. There was no proper script. There were about three hours of orgy footage, featuring none of the principals.

Robinson used his indecision over the ending as a way of keeping Cookie, Irma and Lotte off balance. Would Irma or Lotte be chosen? Or would they combine forces to double-cross Cookie and leave him to his fate? Or would he be allowed to go off with both of them? Robinson didn't care but derived harsh enjoyment from making the others worry. Then, as far as he could, he shot both endings and told me he would make up his mind during the editing and shoot any extra material as necessary. I told him that he might find that more diffi-cult than he imagined.

'What do you mean?'

'Lotte.' I asked him if she had spoken to him. She hadn't. I didn't tell him she was going back to Hamburg. I told him he should speak to her.

The end of filming left everyone irritable and purpose-less. Anti-climax set in during the party afterwards, a dreary, boozy affair with the air of a wake. Repp and Dennis turned up for it, and sat in the corner whisper-ing. All the things that had been held at bay for the last weeks started to seep, then crash over the assembly. Robinson and Lotte quarrelled over her leaving. Robin-son and Cookie fought over the manoeuvres Robinson suspected were going on behind his back: Robinson even volunteered my theory that Cookie, Repp and Dennis were contemplating a move into child pornog-raphy, though where he got that idea I don't know because I'd not mentioned it to him from what I could remember. Repp and Dennis smirked in the back-ground. Toto then threw a tantrum and accused Robinson of ignoring him. That much was true: Toto's role was confined to the kitchen, dreaming up more and more elaborate dishes. (Robinson mopping gravy with a hunk of bread.) In spite of the cocaine, his appetite had not diminished.

Toto embarrassed the party by tearfully declaring, on bended knee, his unrequited love for Robinson and slobbering over the back of his hand. Robinson was invited to tie him up, beat him, anything. I caught Cookie and Repp exchanging glances. Repp then made everyone squirm by standing up and making an insincere speech about what a great crowd we were.

The party dragged on, as incapable of ending as the shooting itself. The mood turned maudlin. Robinson staggered off. I found him in the cutting room, shuttling his scrapbook of images back and forward, staring blankly as the material whizzed by. He looked desolate and in a stage beyond drunkenness. I tried to encourage him, to tell him the film would be all right, everything would be all right. Drink made it hard for me to form my words.

Robinson shrugged, and went back to looking at what he called his death montage. An obsession with statistics ('How many fucks in the history of Soho?') made him wonder how many deaths in the movies. In his despair he sometimes wondered if the porno we made was not, as he had once believed, the opposite of death but merely an alternative, the point at which the circle joined.

Robinson's particular depression that night turned out not to do with work. He was anxious because the cat had vanished, a disappearance that he took for a bad omen. To make him feel better, I suggested we search the building.

We wandered through the violently abandoned set. Debris, unpacked equipment and empty styrofoam cups lay scattered across the room which looked as though it had been fled in an emergency. Upstairs the party finally reached its raucous stage.

We went down to the shooting gallery, neglected since the novelty had worn off. Robinson looked around, hands in pockets, calling the cat's name. He seemed cheered up by my helping. He clasped my shoulder, called me by name. 'Don't worry,' he said. 'It'll all calm down now, you'll see.'

We went upstairs, Robinson wheezing from the effort, and out on to the roof where it was growing light. Robinson continued to call the cat's name. The city below was so quiet it might have been evacuated. Bonfires over in the cardboard shanty town were the only signs of life. These fires were an incongruous detail, given the closeness of the weather. Robinson stared at the skies, watching the anvil hammerheads build, signalling the coming storm. The dank stench of the river a mile away wafted on the hot breeze.

Robinson turned to me. 'Just you and me, like it was at the beginning.'

It started to rain, big, warm splashes that dried almost as soon as they hit the roof. Then came a pause and a distant rumble of thunder. Others from the party came up to watch. The ones too drunk to stand clutched each other for support. Repp and Dennis hovered in the doorway.

The storm was visible from some distance in the approaching dawn, moving in a white wall towards us. Robinson waited in tense anticipation, sober now and alert, no longer the drunken wreck that had sat with me downstairs. The others watched with a mixture of fear and wonder, their faces lit pale by the first bolts of lightning. We should have seen this storm as evidence of forces larger than us, though none did. Each of us believed – I could read it on our faces – that we were the cause, that our ritual ceremonies of the last weeks had invoked it, and this deluge was the dramatic result of our efforts.

When the rain hit, visibility fell to a few feet. Lightning lit up the immediate vicinity a sickly yellow. The
rain fell like a warm douche, its noise drowning out all
other sound except the cracks of thunder now overhead.
I lost sight of the others, glimpsing the silhouette of
Robinson at the parapet whenever lightning struck. A
small group started yelping to make themselves heard
above the storm. Lightning hit a nearby building.

The effect of the storm was strangely benign and in-
sulating. It washed away the exhaustion of the last
weeks. I felt my way forward like a blind man, turning
this way and that until pleasantly giddy. My thoughts
flickered sporadically, little bursts of illumination trig-
gered in my skull by the tracery of lightning, flashes of
clarity that for tiny moments lit up the surrounding
gloom. I lacked Robinson's grand vision, his appetite
and application, I knew that. I saw the extent to which I
had been his dupe, and corrupted. Another flash. I saw
that I had lacked the character to resist. I saw how I had
sought refuge in our collaborations in the hope they
might open doors that otherwise would have remained
closed. I saw too that I had attributed to Robinson skills
of navigation he didn't possess, that far from the epic
voyage with its landfall at the end that he had promised,
we were becalmed and drifting. An exhilarating resentment poured over me, giving me strength to decide.

A face loomed out of the storm, and slid past. I
reached a chimney stack and edged round. Rain was falling even more thickly. I felt quite alone.

A flash of lightning provided a split-second picture of
Robinson and Lotte. They were locked in an embrace,
using the chimney stack for support. Her legs, white and
slick with wet, were spread, her skirt rucked up to
accommodate him. Her face rested on his shoulder, pale.
Her mouth formed a perfect O as she greedily drank in
the rain, her tongue flicking in and out. Her eyes were

closed. Robinson thrust at her, his libido restored.

My certainty of a few moments earlier fell away. I was a child again, excluded from the secret games of others, always more interesting than one's own. I saw Robinson and Lotte, fused together, then the curtain of rain hid them again. Thunder cracked, still overhead.

I sat down. I'd had enough. Maybe Lotte would stumble across me later and the spirit of the storm would make her give herself to me too. Rain beat on my skull, ran down my neck, under my arms, and I fancied I heard the thin cry of Lotte's climax.

The storm moved on, the shapes of the rooftop returned by degrees. I was the last one left. The others had gone. The rain had cleansed the city, making it look etched and graphic. The sharpness of the air brought with it the freshness of new resolutions. Day moved in from the east. I stayed on the roof. Gradually the others came out too, even Repp and Dennis. We watched in silence as the panorama took on colour, shades of grey at first, then the bone white of the brick.

No one missed Lotte, not until Robinson asked. Someone thought she was downstairs asleep. Robinson went to fetch her. He thought she would want to be there.

I spotted her first. I failed to recognise her at once. She looked like some weird, indecipherable symbol or sign – a little like a Manx herald – spread out on the pavement.

We found her strangely unmarked. Robinson was fetched, then a blanket. Lotte was carried inside, shoulder high as by pall bearers, and laid on the table in the kitchen. Robinson asked to be left alone with her.

The mood among the rest of us was edgy and erratic. Hangovers were setting in. More drink was got to counter the shock of our discovery. The earlier keyed-up mood of the party returned, in spite of the release of the storm. Toto subsided into drunken, hysterical laughter, I kept repeating to myself: she came and she went, and had to suppress a fit of giggles. For the first time in ages I wanted to look at myself in a mirror. Had Robinson been her angel of death? That old association between sex and death, the spasm of the former a rehearsal for the latter. Had Robinson fixed one to follow the other? Had he, in other words, chucked her off the roof when he had done with her?

When Robinson had first come out into the street to where Lotte lay he had looked surprised but calm. I saw him squint up at the building tops, bathed in golden light, then both ways down the street, still in shadow, as if to calculate the effect of the light in terms of shooting a scene. The gutters were flooded. Patches of dry were already starting to appear on the pavement as the heat descended again. The only sound came from the gurgle of the drains. We huddled silently around Lotte. For a moment or two the scene took on a sacrificial air, then Repp, in panicky tones, suggested we call the police. Robinson overrode him and told us to take Lotte inside.

It was also Robinson who decided that the death would remain unreported. Lotte was laid out in the kitchen for the rest of the day, surrounded by a shrine of candles, then taken out and buried under cover of darkness.

During the day, Robinson went down alone to the cardboard city. He described it as a sea of mud. The inhabitants who were left were caked brown with it, their flimsy shelters for the most part flattened. Many had moved on. Lotte's death made Robinson reckless; I half-expected him not to return. Whether or not he had killed her – deliberately or by accident – he was overwhelmed with grief.

Lotte was buried on the outskirts of the cardboard

city, in a hole that Robinson paid for to be dug and filled. For a hearse we used Cookie's old Volvo estate, the one I vaguely inherited when he lost his licence. She was buried with little ceremony. In the end, it was just Cookie, Robinson and me. A light drizzle fell and the ground was still a quagmire from the storm. Manoeuvring the body from the back of the Volvo to the grave took a lot of slithering and lurching and swearing. I didn't like the whole thing, dumping her like that, and the chance of getting picked up by a police patrol; it wasn't my idea of how things should be done.

We stood around the open grave at a loss for any gesture or words. Then, unprompted, Cookie started to sing 'Amazing Grace'. Robinson told him to stop. Cookie ignored him. His voice soared and Robinson, upstaged, turned away and walked back to the car. Cookie stood ram-rod straight and saluted as he finished singing. I found myself crying.

Back at the factory Robinson retreated into his room, and scarcely ventured out for a week. I spent much of that time in St John's Wood, rebuilding my marriage, preparing for what I thought of as a new identity. Rather in the way I had once invested all my hopes in Robinson I now devoted them to my wife. For all the traumas of the recent past, I felt in better shape than I had for a long time. I seemed to have shaken off the depression that had lain waiting to ambush me for most of my life. Perhaps something had been confronted and overcome.

When Robinson emerged he went back to making routine porno movies like Repp wanted, with no ambition. The personnel at the factory quickly changed. Stefan was gone, a replacement for Lotte was found by Repp. Irma was relegated to behind the camera again, at Repp's insistence. Whenever Repp talked to him Robinson stuck his hands in his pockets and looked a million miles away. 'Whatever you say, old man,' he said with great weariness and no trace of his former irony.

The only point at which he dug in his heels was on the matter of finishing the last film. Repp talked to him about completing it as a memorial to Lotte. Cookie, who fancied himself as an actor, was vain about the project and wanted it done for that reason. Robinson procrastinated, and whenever we got into the cutting room he ignored the film and sat there adding to his scrapbook of images. Sometimes he sought my encouragement, and like a nurse with a mental patient I praised his meaningless, broken jumble of images, cut anyhow, as though it were his masterpiece.

The last material of Lotte which Robinson had shot, of her laid out on the kitchen table and lit by candles, invariably moved him to tears. By night, he sat at that same table, smoothing its surface with his hand, trying to find some trace of her. He took fewer drugs, which loosened Cookie's hold over him, but still drank himself into a stupor. The nights of scouring the streets appeared to be over. I wondered how long before Repp got rid of him. I warned Robinson to watch his back but he didn't care.

I studied his face for signs of his knowledge about the fate of Lotte. Once I asked him if he had been with her when she fell. He gave a look of such anguish that I hadn't the heart to press him. My instinct was to give him the benefit of the doubt: he was genuinely bereft without her, so much so that I realised I understood nothing of the complexity of the relationship. Later I qualified that, and kept an open verdict.

In the end, I made do with the version I imagined Robinson constructed for himself, true or false: that, after being with him, she had crossed to the edge of the roof and he had lost sight of her. In a moment of exhilaration she had taken the railing in both hands and leaned out until she was on tiptoe, then, startled perhaps by a crack of thunder, she had lost her balance and toppled over. Yes, and the thin cry of her fall is what I heard. As I pushed her, I want to add, except I didn't, though I would have done, gladly, if I could have changed places with Robinson to be with her for her final coming.

I held my breath and counted the days. We were living through a period of psychic brutality, brought about by a combination of Lotte's death and the strange weather. A tropical rain fell over London day after day without relief. The rains penetrated the building, both via the roof and up through the cellar. Soon the shooting range was under several inches of water, and damp stains started to appear on the walls upstairs, sinister Rorschach patterns that mapped our disintegrating psyches. Guns lay scattered around like props, waiting to be used.

Robinson spent more and more time alone in his room, slumped in front of a monitor, occasionally scribbling notes for his scrapbook. I saw some of them. They were indecipherable squiggles. His hands shook so much he could barely write. His life once again was measured in lines of drugs, supplied by Cookie. Robinson went through elaborate tests to establish their purity. He suspected Cookie of doctoring them with laxative. His digestive system was completely shot and he complained of shitting water most of the time. Unemptied ashtrays overflowed with his cigar butts.

At St John's Wood there was a hiccough. My wife became nervous about our living together again, feeling that the crazy hours I was keeping, working on the film, made it impossible. Also, with the rains travel was becoming increasingly difficult.

I'd had to abandon the Volvo. A petrol shortage, which had not been there a fortnight earlier, turned into a crisis in days. Certain garages were designated to carry stocks, the rest closed down. It took an hour or more to get to the head of a queue, then all too often the supply dried up a car or so too soon. Tempers ran high during these endless waits and it felt like a short step to lawlessness.

Rumours went around of petrol pirates who drove elaborately fendered trucks to smash their way past cars to the pumps. These commando-style raids were usually executed by armed masked men, so the story went. A further embellishment to these tales was the police ambush and shoot-outs with bystanders mown down and petrol explosions. It was difficult to get confirmation of these skirmishes. The television news pretended nothing unusual was going on. Incidents were isolated, connections left unmade. Once, on a local late-night news slot, I saw a reference to a garage attack, as though it were a solitary occurrence.

Only the weather forecasters made any analysis. The weather became the news. It was the worst weather on record. Pictures of reservoirs bursting their banks replaced the more familiar ones of drought. London was discreetly put on flood alert though no one paid much attention. Minor officials and major politicians were interviewed to reassure us that the problems – of transport, fuel, supply – were at the point of being solved by teams of drafted specialists working round the clock.

Gaps started to appear in the tube circuit. Between King's Cross and Baker Street was closed for some days. This made getting to St John's Wood difficult. Journeys were abruptly terminated or became delayed for several hours while trains waited in tunnels. Passengers grew rebellious in the clammy heat.

People started carrying little emergency packs, freezer

bags in which they kept cold flannels to revive themselves. With the humidity nobody dressed formally any
more. Instead they looked as though they were on safari,
in their shorts and vests, their provisions in little
pouches strapped to their waists. Their clothes were a
sign that crossing the city had ceased to be a normal
journey and now had to be regarded as an epic trek.

I gave myself a deadline to finish assembling Lotte's last
film. I wanted to see it through, for some reason I could
not explain, and a week more flat out ought to do it. I
explained this patiently to Robinson to try and steer him
to thinking about the ending. 'Whatever you say, old
man.'

He left me to cut the film alone. I felt blind in front of
the material. I imposed an order but some inner rhythm
of Robinson's eluded me, the true sense of it perhaps. I
felt that behind the images I was assembling on the
screen lay a shadow film – sharp and clear and waiting to
be peeled off by the right hands – that was beyond my
limited skill.

I appealed to Robinson but he was obsessed with his
scrapbook. Only with this did he rouse himself, did his
monologues crackle in the way they once had. I veered
between scepticism and belief whenever he talked about
it. From what I could see of the material it was not even
intelligible, but it gave him back some confidence, in-
spired him even, and for that I was relieved. I thought of
the Robinson of old, and tried to chart his breakdown.
Only when he worked on his scrapbook did I see the remaining flickers of his cabbalistic energy. His ironic
eyebrow made one of its now rare appearances as he
likened his effort to that of the alchemists of Prague.

I was desperate to leave, but I couldn't. These last
lines had to be played out, and once the obligation had

been fulfilled (to Lotte, she was why) then a new start could be made. One more week, I told my wife, that's all I was asking, then, if she could find the time, perhaps we could go away somewhere, together. We agreed on the week. She would wait that long. 'The last time I will,' she said, as we said good-bye at the door. The hall behind her beckoned, a picture of a civilised world I had long abandoned. I almost changed my mind and asked her to take me in again. The thought of another week of exile was more than I could take. Thin rain slanted down, illuminated by the haloes of street-lamps.

I walked through the wet night back to Clerkenwell, not wanting to risk getting stuck underground. Walking away from my wife, back to Robinson, just as I would soon walk away from him and return to her, to where the forking paths of my life would rejoin. Down Abbey Road and Lisson Grove to the Euston Road, past King's Cross, up the Gray's Inn Road to Rosebery Avenue and Farringdon, the city as deserted as one under curfew, cars abandoned where they had run out of petrol. Broken glass lay like scattered jewels on a pavement in Clerkenwell, a shop window broken by vandals. Seven more days.

Radio stations that played old hits stuck to their regular, hourly bulletins. To listen to them you'd think everything was normal. Then the rain suddenly stopped and a pale sunlight shone for a few hours. After so much for so long, the absence of the noise of rain was uncanny.

Up on the roof, I had made a little shrine where Lotte had fallen – a few sprigs in an old milk bottle – and had taken to going up there. Since her death no one used the roof. I watched the city drying out, in what seemed like minutes. Then the sun, seeming too fragile to last, dimmed and vanished behind a haze that grew into a thick fog rolling in from the east. It looked like smoke from a fire, billowing over the distant rooftops and obliterating everything in its path.

As the fog closed in, there came a strange screeching, like the clouds were scratching the buildings as they enveloped them. Then I saw, in hazy silhouette, thousands of seagulls caught up in the path of the fog. Many of the gulls had reached a point of exhaustion, and were flopping to rest on roofs. I counted twenty on ours alone.

The next day the gulls were still there, like sentinels, and the fog too, reducing visibility to a few yards.

One gull became trapped in the building, and was either unable or reluctant to escape in spite of windows being left open. A walk through the factory became like being in a suspense film: peripheral movement, unexpected flurry, the lurch of the heart, the screech. The beating of the wings of death.

The endless porno conveyor belt came to resemble the meat-processing part of the factory. An Alsatian dog took to roaming the buildings, not the only one to take refuge in the factory, but the only one to feature in one of Robinson's films, wanked off by a youth with a missing tooth and dirty fingernails. Shooting proceeded at the same intense rate, except now too much energy was expended. Too many things started to go wrong. Someone was badly electrocuted. Equipment was stolen. Robinson moved as silent as a broken ghost through it all.

Like a prisoner – except I wasn't, I was free to leave – I sat in my hutch-like space, scratching off the days. For that last week I kept a diary that I hid behind my table, less for the record, more as a way of telling myself that all this would end.

My dreams were punctuated by the flapping wings of the seagull, its yellow beak predatory, and the loping trot of the Alsatian, tongue lolling. I awoke thinking of

Robinson devouring himself, thought of how I could save him.

In the end I provoked him instead, deliberately, by taking over on the set one morning, at Repp's insistence, after Robinson failed to appear. When he turned up and saw what was happening, he strode in a fury across the floor. He screamed at me, accusing me again of betraying him. I started to walk away, and he span me round and hit me across the face. In the split second before his hand connected I saw that I'd been in a trance, like being under a spell, since the slapping of Lotte.

That night we sat together and cut our own separate pictures as though nothing had happened. I added the slap to the tower of slights and resentments I was building up against him, all of which I listed carefully in my diary.

On day five of my countdown the fog disappeared and the rain came back, shading the sky. The damp stain in my room, starved of nourishment, grew spectacularly in the space of hours.

On day four, feeling hemmed in, I suggested Robinson and I went out for a drink. Robinson looked agitated at the thought and shook his head saying he couldn't possibly. The nearest pub was only three streets away, I argued. Robinson just shook his head and said, 'No, no, no.' This a man who was prepared almost to strangle a boy for the sake of some tape experiment. He qualified himself by saying there was too much work to do, he couldn't possibly. By my reckoning, Robinson hadn't been outside the factory since the burial of Lotte. I had no idea when he had last seen daylight. The set was sealed off from it, and his room always had the curtains drawn.

'Please,' I said, pointing at the film I was cutting. 'I'm begging you, let's finish this so I can go.'

He looked at me with great sadness. 'Is that what you want?'

'Yes.'

He held my face in his hands for a long time before turning back to his work.

Day three, two to go, I wrote in the diary. That evening Robinson came to me, more sober than in a long time. 'I have made up my mind,' he said. 'Tomorrow we finish Lotte's film.' His hand went into his pocket and the aluminium container was produced, flipped in the air and caught with his other hand. He grinned, his old grin.

'We'll drive out to Denver Sluice, just the three of us – you, me and Cookie – and do the scene at first light.' Robinson was to play a gangster. He had established himself in a couple of scenes in the film, already shot. He wanted me to operate the camera and gave me a list of shots. 1. Long shot of the car drawing up. 2. Closer angle of stationary car from low down (masking the fact there was no driver, and no second gangster as in the outline) showing Cookie and Robinson getting out. 3. Wide angle covering their walk from car to canal. 4 and 5. Final close-ups of Robinson and Cookie.

We checked over the camera. I felt nervous. I'd not used one before except for our basement tapes. Robinson told me not to worry.

We took the Volvo. Robinson set up a light in the car because he wanted to film a close-up of Cookie as we drove.

He seemed more like his former self: washed, neat, shaven, hair combed back. Cookie kept fussing that we weren't doing it properly with just the three of us. Robinson assured him we would pick up the shots we needed. 'Your big moment. Don't want a lot of hangers-on around. Do we, old man?' Robinson was in the front seat, twisted round and filming Cookie, who sounded nervous. 'Bit outside my range, this.'

'Nothing to it. If it looks no good we'll do it again.'

We moved out into the suburbs, close by where I had once lived, up the A41 with its litany of unevocative names – Colindale, Burnt Oak, Edgware, Stanmore – and across to the A1, more names, more rain. The beat of windscreen wipers, the smear of traffic film decreasing visibility, half a tank of petrol, not enough to get there and back.

'Once had a wife who came from Elstree,' Cookie said, surprised to be reminded of it. There had been four wives altogether, maybe five. The fifth he was vague about because he had been on a bender in Nevada at the time, and neither of them was quite sure if they had gone through with the ceremony or just talked about it. 'Anyway,' said Cookie swigging from the bottle that Robinson passed him. 'We were in one of those places where they have twenty-four-hour wedding chapels so we could easily.'

Robinson kept on filming while Cookie reminisced. He told Cookie to keep the bottle. 'You can't use any of this stuff of me rabbiting on,' Cookie pointed out.

'It doesn't matter. Carry on. It's interesting.'

The countryside was flatter and I fancied it was getting lighter outside. 'I'm nervous about this,' Cookie announced again. 'Shagging on camera, no problem. Treat it as a bonus. What's your total, old man?' he said looking at Robinson. His voice was starting to slur. 'Shagged a lot, have you? Sometime wish I'd kept score, compared it with the Guinness Book of Records, 'cept they don't list that sort of stuff. List fucking everything else.' He paused and belched. 'Never actually been to Nevada. It was just the four. Bit of embellishment. Nothing wrong with that.'

Robinson kept taping in spite of Cookie's protests. 'Don't want any of this stuff, won't be able to use it.' He dozed off for a while and Robinson still continued to tape.

We turned off the highway and drove east into the Fens down desolate, flat roads that ran straight as an arrow until you decided they ran that way for ever and met a vicious bend. 'Steady on,' said Cookie as we slewed around one of these corners. I remembered a scene of drunk driving in a movie (I was drunk), couldn't think of the film.

There was almost no traffic and I drove on full beam, dipping for the occasional car that trundled past, never in any hurry. The rain stopped. Robinson and I sat in silence. Cookie fumbled in his sleep and woke up trying to work out where he was. Robinson seemed calmer than I had known him in a long time. I remembered the movie: Richard Burton in *Who's Afraid of Virginia Woolf?* – a hammy drunken actor trying to play an un-hammy drunk.

We arrived at Denver Sluice as the light came up on a landscape that looked like a child's unfinished drawing: a huge sky bisected by the line of the land, the network of canals – oily as sluggish mercury in the coming light – converging on the sluice whose churning waters sounded disconcerting and alien in such inanimate sur-roundings.

Robinson was suddenly on edge. 'Hurry, we haven't much time.' We drove around looking for a suitable spot. Robinson got out. A gust of raw weather blew into the car as he shut the door. I watched him, framed in the windscreen, while he found his camera positions. He finally settled on a stretch of canal bank identical to the rest, apart from a solitary, thin sapling. He waved his arm, summoning me out. I was reluctant to leave the warm fug of the car. Cookie hunched miserably in the back. The rain was holding off, but there was a cold wind. 'Don't fancy catching my death of cold,' he grum-bled. Robinson waved his arm again, impatiently. I got out and walked over to him. 'Hurry!' he insisted.

He talked me through the shots again, gabbling them off. 'We've twenty minutes at the most before full daylight.'

We shot in sequence. For the shot of the car's arrival I had to switch on the camera and run back to the car to drive it into frame. Then we did the low angle of the car door as it opens, when Cookie is pushed out, followed by Robinson, and both leave frame. Their progress from the car to the canal I filmed from the bank, panning with them until canal and tree are revealed. Cookie stumbled convincingly on the way up, probably the brandy. At the top of the bank Robinson shoved him forwards and down on to his knees. He then turned and called to me, 'Quick, do his close-up. No, make it full figure, then move in on the face.'

We quarrelled about that until Robinson screamed at me to just do it. I picked up the camera, to get a better angle. Robinson shouted at me, 'Do it on the fucking zoom, we don't have time.' Cookie said something about having a last fag, ha ha, and Robinson repeated impatiently that there wasn't time, he could have one later. I set up. Robinson took a hurried look through the frame, made a final adjustment, went to his position and called action.

Cookie started to turn round, as though he'd just thought of something. The gun in Robinson's hand gave a dry cough and Cookie pitched forward awkwardly and lay face down in the earth.

I thought it hadn't looked very good and told them to go again, quickly, before it got too light. It was my turn to shout. Robinson ignored me. He was breathing deeply, in the grip of some strong emotion. I adjusted the frame and filmed him like that, thinking it might help in the editing, then repeated what I'd said. 'Come on, before it gets too light. We can get it better. Perhaps Cookie can slow down the fall.'

Robinson said, 'It's fine. Anyway, it's too late now.' Sun broke through the clouds, low on the horizon, bathing his face in the softest of lights. Still filming him, I yelled at him to look at the light, told him it was there for us.

Robinson looked triumphant and helpless at the same time. I pulled back to a wide shot. Cookie lay hunched on the ground. The sight of his knees so awkwardly bent made me realise what we had just done. What I'd been filming was Robinson putting a live round into Cookie's head: we had shot our ending.

In that instant I also understood that Robinson did not intend what we had just done for Lotte's film. He wanted it for his own crazy quilt of images in his meaningless scrapbook. I could see from his face that he now believed that he had the shot that made sense of everything, the one shot that, when placed right, would illuminate and give meaning to all the others.

Robinson had it all worked out. There were weights in the boot of the car for Cookie's body. I ignored his demands for help. Instead I filmed on.

I filmed the approaching rain, a visible band that advanced across the flat, black fields towards us. I filmed the rain altering Cookie's appearance, plastering his hair flat against his skull. For a moment he came alive, the one eye half open and the splashing rain making it wink. The mouth, snapped back to reveal teeth, was similarly animated: Cookie's last grimace turned into a ghostly, flashing smile. There was a wash of pink where water mingled with blood.

I filmed Robinson awkwardly manipulating the body to attach the weights. The rain fell, and it was darker now than when we had shot Cookie, almost too dark to film. I shot the canal's spattered and broken surface, shot the brown mud scar in the grass where Cookie had slipped, shot the mist closing in, blurring the distant line of trees until they were gone, shot the landscape as it broke up into flat, abstract planes, green, brown, grey and black. EXT. FENS DAY – Close-up, Robinson's black Oxfords as he shoves Cookie's body with a toe-cap (while my own shoes filled with water).

Rain blurred the lens, smearing the image, but I filmed on. Cookie's body rolled once, then stuck. Robinson, grunting from the exertion, had to use his hands to push the body down the bank. It rolled, straight at first then off at an angle (I lost it in the viewfinder for a moment and cursed). Cookie went into the water with a brief splash. The ripples were soon lost in the disturbance of the rain on the canal's surface. Close-up, Robinson's face, a low angle: heroic and flawed, taking a corny line and making it great. 'So long. Old man.'

I filmed him walking back to the car. There was nothing to say. We had gone beyond words, had travelled too far together. These and other clichés filled my head.

I saw how we had made literal a language of technology: shooting became a shooting, the final shot being just that. Robinson, more than me, had also recognised a wider process of acceleration, and his insight had a visionary dimension. He had once told me how private behaviour would be increasingly monitored, not by the state, but by people themselves. Technological advance would be accompanied by private lines of retreat, a withdrawal. Access to this new ubiquitous technology meant experience and memory were no longer enough, now that it was possible to have a personal visual souvenir. Being able to reduce everything to an act of replay, or to a freeze-frame, being able to turn everything into television – divorced from oneself – carried its own absolution. As such, I realised, Cookie's death had little to do with me or Robinson. It had been absorbed into a larger whole and now belonged with the enormous scrapbook of tape Robinson had made and whose possibilities I began to grasp for the first time.

I only minded about Cookie being shot in that I wished I didn't feel so flat about it. It was over. We were done, and I could go home. Robinson could finish the project himself.

We got to the car. Robinson stood there in the rain as I filmed on. 'You drive, old man,' he said and got in the passenger side. (I remember once writing: Such fine tuning of the social itinerary was typical of him, and I never did mind, much.) I filmed him in profile through the window, looking like a gangster in a Jean-Pierre Melville film. Just one more shot, I decided, from away in the landscape, of the car. I looked at Robinson through the windscreen. The rain softened his features, made him look young again.

('*You drive, old man.*' What if I didn't? The scenario perhaps had a twist I'd not seen before.)

I kept walking, away from the car until it was only just visible in the mist. I made the shot and wondered if I were right. I stood a long time looking. Robinson became impatient. He leaned over and punched the horn. He got out and shouted after me, his voice curiously lifeless in the mist and the drumming of the rain. This time, I told myself, I'd ride out my hunch. A long, angry blast sounded on the horn, followed by a handful of exasperated short bursts.

There then followed a strange shooting: me shooting him shooting at me. He stood at the car tracking my departure with his pistol. He'd be lucky, I thought, to hit me at that distance. I heard a couple of thin cracks. Perhaps one or two of the puddle splashes were caused by rounds from the gun. I raised the camera and taped a burst of him, in extreme long shot, next to the car in the rain. As he got in behind the wheel, I pushed the zoom to maximum and closed in for a last shot of his face through the rain-blurred windscreen. The image was grainy and breaking up, pockmarked and ravaged. I watched the huge moon face search the dashboard for clues, frustration showing as he fiddled hopefully with knobs and levers. He started the engine. The car lurched (through the viewfinder it looked as though Robinson had been hit from behind with some force) and stopped. I was right. Robinson did not drive. Robinson was stuck. (*Conquered in a car seat.*)

He gave it a couple more goes. As I moved on and the car vanished into the mist I heard the engine cough and die, cough and die. I walked on. The car door slammed. Once or twice I saw him loom out of the mist in the distance, a tiny figure weaving his uncertain way, lurching like a drunk. He was too unfit to catch up. My last image of him is almost invisible, a ghostly silhouette, slipping as he climbed a wire fence and collapsing on the other side, one arm aloft, his fist hanging on to the wire.

I found a road. It was straight and flat, the unchanging landscape an endless grid of drainage canals and black fields. No cars passed. There was a line of trees on the edge of the mist and I counted them as a way of marking progress. Sometimes the road disappeared under water, and the surrounding fields became lakes. Then the landscape was gone altogether, leaving me with nothing except a feeling of acute physical discomfort. I was wet to the skin and shivering. Blisters grew on my heels.

A single car came and went, coming out of the mist too late for me to flag it down, its engine noise muffled again quickly by the fog.

I saw Cookie inert on his canal bed, dead but for his eyes which took in the dim light of the surface above him. I saw Robinson hanging on the wire. The camera lay cradled inside my coat.

The first village I came to was completely shut up. I banged on a door; no one came. A light on in a tiny police station made me hurry on.

Some miles further along was a railway station, little more than a halt. It was closed up as well. (Sometimes I fancied I heard convoys of trucks moving in the distance.) I had no idea how long I had been walking. My watch had stopped, as usual. There was a telephone box to one side of the station and I called the operator and asked the time (early afternoon) and made her call the St John's Wood number on a reverse charge. 'Caller, are you there?' Her nose sounded blocked. I imagined her warm behind double-glazing and drowsy in an over-heated, airless office. 'Caller? I'm getting no answer at present.' She hung up before I could ask about the state of the trains.

I decided to push on. The fog lifted a little. An incline brought some tiny relief to the monotony of the land-scape, but made walking more painful. The top of the rise revealed only more of the same: the canal network, saturated earth, trees – always in the distance – a line of frozen detonations in the mist, visibility clearing enough to see a road far ahead, cutting across mine, and the pin-prick lights of a passing vehicle.

Rain turned to drizzle and the wind changed. Fog closed in again thicker than ever. At the crossroads I turned off and soon after turned again, asphalt and sod-den verge my only bearings. I was going home is what I told myself and the first place I get to I'll find a taxi to take me all the way back to London. Is what I told myself.

Another desolate village, again shut up, appeared, per-haps the same one as before and I had merely gone round in a circle. A general store had a little clock sign showing it closed at five. I rattled the door but no one answered. Apart from the store, the main street consisted of stunted terrace houses. There was a pub as mean as the houses, closed also. When I banged on the door, a dog barked. I pictured the landlord on top of his wife upstairs as they fucked their way to opening time.

At the end of the village stood a house alone. A sign in the window said: *Vacancies*. A skinny girl of fifteen maybe came to the door and said, 'Twelve pound fifty.' She showed no curiosity at the state of me. I shook uncontrollably.

A cot-like bed waited in the tomb-like room at the top of narrow stairs. The girl insisted I pay in advance and for a moment I wondered if these were the preliminaries to a sexual transaction. I handed over almost the last of my cash and half-expected her to start undressing. She pocketed the money, said breakfast was until 8.15, and the toilet and bath were down the hall, with hot water on a meter.

The central light was on when I awoke (I didn't remember it being on earlier). I was delirious, and for all I knew I had caught my death of cold (Cookie's phrase, I remembered).

Perhaps I did die. No one paid me any attention after that, didn't appear to notice me. I came to, after I don't know how long, feeling papery and so light-headed that my body seemed no longer to be mine. I watched myself as one does a stranger, curious to see what he will do next. The camera was still under the bed. My clothes were dry, and I dressed and left, seeing no one.

Outside it had stopped raining, though the street was still wet. I walked back the length of the empty village. At the far end was a bus shelter with a group of children standing. When a bus eventually came I got on last. The driver ignored me (looked straight through me), asked for no fare. I sat down at the back and fell asleep again.

In between dozing I was feverish and my mind wandered.

The bus ground on across the flat landscape, hidden now behind condensation on the windows. The children got off at some point and when I next looked there were half a dozen new passengers. I dreamed of the souls of the recently departed, in transit. I wondered why the coach didn't smell more of damp, given the moist warmth. (I couldn't smell anything, I realised.) The linoleum aisle was wet with muddy footprints. I filmed with the camera a bit, without anyone noticing. I still thought I was going home.

The bus came to a terminus in a town with a railway station, and we all got off. I was feeling bad again, not myself at all. Speaking to anyone appeared to be out of the question. Perhaps I was suffering from delayed shock and had gone dumb for the moment.

The station ticket office was closed, but chalked on a board was a timetable of the reduced service, and instructions to pay on the train.

I waited an hour for a train due in half that time. The rain came back. Oil on railway sleepers glistened in wet, dying light. (I filmed that.) My shivering returned. How much time had passed since Robinson? Infernal rain.

I slept all the way to London. No one asked for the fare. The coins I had left were enough for a ticket to St John's Wood. It was night when I arrived.

She had left, of course. The time had elapsed. She had been quite precise. For all I knew, I was a week past the deadline, though I thought three or four days more likely. (How long had I lain in that room?) What did it matter? She was gone. The house was dark and locked. I contemplated breaking in and waiting, but there was no point. I went back to the factory. I had the key to that.

The factory was empty too. Most of the equipment was gone, presumably moved on by Repp and Dennis to the next enterprise. Only the editing room was untouched, safe behind its padlock. In the kitchen the milk looked sour by several days (again no smell). I wondered about Robinson.

How long I stayed I don't know. I wasn't well, I knew that. My mind slipped in and out of hallucination. The few times I felt hungry I took from a stock of tins in the kitchen. What was real hardly mattered any more: imagination and memory bled into each other to take on an existence independent of myself. Even Robinson I began to think of as a figment of my imagination, the daring alternative to myself.

These are the things that frightened me: the thin crack of black beyond a door left ajar. Damp sheets on the unmade bed in the studio, which I took to sleeping in. The beating wings of the seagull upstairs. The pack of mangy dogs that now roamed the factory. I took to carrying a gun. The Alsatian I shot when I found it barring the way to the editing room, snarling and drooling saliva. The other dogs fed off its carcass.

I forced myself to go up to the roof to look for signs of life in the rest of the city. Lights still went on and off, but fewer it seemed, and further away now.

Rain fell incessantly, sometimes no more than the finest of drizzles, more usually a monotonous downpour. Damp patches took over more of the building. I kept meaning to put buckets down in the studio to catch the leaks. Water now reached the bottom of the stairs. The weather seemed to be having a strange effect on my body, which felt permanently damp. I noticed I didn't need to shave any more. My nails, however, had started to grow faster.

When I was up to it, I worked on Robinson's scrapbook, cutting it as I thought he would have wished.

There was a mountain of material I had not seen before, taken off television, and boxes of other tapes from his collection. I contemplated what was put before me, searching for a pattern. A scratchy fragment of black and white film of a group of men being slowly hanged. The final privacy of the torture room, with electrodes and a taped interrogation in Spanish. The end of Cookie too. I cut it all together with as much reverence as I could, this monument to torment. I began to see in it the beginnings of a Grand Design.

I had lucid conversations with Lotte in the kitchen, in which we began over and said all the things we should have said. I heard my wife talking in other rooms, but she had always moved on when I looked for her. There were happy times, some of which I filmed. Lotte and I in the kitchen. But there was a fault on the tape. It registered only inanimate objects, and Lotte and I were left off, just our voices remained. I grew pleased with these shots of empty rooms and cut them into the master tape.

Babette the cat I found in the shooting range, which lay well under water. Who was responsible for her death I couldn't decide. Sometimes I thought it was Cookie, as a curse on Robinson. Other times, I blamed the inhabitants of the cardboard city. Perhaps they were about to eat it and were disturbed. Yes that was it. Otherwise why go to the trouble of shaving and disembowelling it? Maybe it was Robinson after all, tempting fate.

Sometimes I drove myself out to wander the city in search of my wife. Bank cash machines still functioned, a sign that some things outside were still working, though the transport system had packed up entirely. The house in St John's Wood stayed shut. I filmed it and filmed my steps back to the earlier house where we had lived together.

I walked through the centre of the city, those parts that were still negotiable. The bookshop was half-gone, all the books in the basement damaged by flood. Veronica had a sign in the window saying their shop was temporarily closed. Repp and Dennis's office, in the mews off Wardour Street, was for sale, the building patrolled by guard dogs. I looked in the lit windows of restaurants for her, knowing that these were the last of our days. I saw myself caught in some kind of time slip – an invisible crevice – watching helpless as she sat down to dine with Robinson. Jaunty, ironic Robinson. Robinson of 'Ah fuck your wife.'

I saw cracks in the pavement of Meard Street; I watched Humphrey Bogart dying in *High Sierra*; saw a hand clutching a number eight bus ticket. I searched the tapes for some sign of my wife, a shot, a picture of her that would lock the material in place, and finally make sense of it, for me, but found none.

Other images came instead. Many of them I cut into Robinson's film. I saw a woman swinging out her right arm. William Blake walking down Poland Street, shadowed by a dog. The gunmen waiting on the grassy knoll. I saw all the doors in my life (save those with her). Blind Borges wrote: *I saw a tattered labyrinth (it was London)*. I saw myself as a child standing at a window and the shadow of my mother, her voice saying, 'Come away now'; Cookie and the sly look of the wild, feral girl. A moving walkway at Gatwick airport; tank manoeuvres in the desert. I saw the children I never had; Marlene Dietrich telling Orson Welles, 'Your future's all used up.' Traffic lights changing in empty streets. Lee Marvin walking through LAX, his footsteps like gunshots. I watched a game show host position his guests on the camera mark. A Texaco station on a road out of Felixstowe, overhead a jet plane on its penultimate flight before crashing. I saw Germaine Greer fuck Warren

Beatty; Lotte and Iain on the sofa; a first edition of *For Love and Hunger*. I saw Princess Diana's sideways look to her husband on her wedding night. Broken glass on the hard shoulder, train tracks running east to Poland. I saw a photograph of Rainer Werner Fassbinder directing *Veronica Voss*, watched George Best send a goalkeeper the wrong way. In the wake of a power cruiser, children run on Hampstead Heath. Test crash footage of wired-up dummies in cars. Brendan Behan drunk and roaring, 'At least I don't fuck my own dogs.' The wall against which the Ceausescus were shot. Weeds on a building site; the rolling credits of a TV comedy (the last one); the slap of the Thames against London Bridge. Cars cruise high above the narrative. The pavement outside the Magdala Tavern. Robinson in Dresden. Dirk Bogarde shopping alone. A dropped glove. The only person not laughing in an audience. A tie my father wore. Engine oil stains and painted white lines on concrete. A line of poplars on Bredon Hill. A woman hoovers in a tower block. Shop dummies float in the Grand Caledonian canal. The hum of an empty refrigerator. Ruth Ellis's botched hanging, the one that Pierrepoint wouldn't talk about. A smile of invitation never followed up. A politician lying. Tweezers on a dressing table. I saw the false entries in Donald Crowhurst's log. A line from a song: *Much older now, with hat on, drinking wine*. The white chalked outline of a body, once mine, on a pavement, from on high, the chalk blurring in the rain.

Quite suddenly the city was reprieved by an Indian summer of cloudless blue skies. People started to appear again. The air was one of carnival. It became a habit to stroll down to the river's edge, wading through flooded streets, to watch the flotilla of boats that paraded defiantly up and down. Boat parties became fashionable and the whole city took to the water for long festive evenings of drunken carousing. The mood remained light and buoyant, as though some victory had been achieved.

I took the camera out, along with one of the pistols left over from the shooting range, anticipating that I would find Robinson. Together we would restage the shooting of Lee Harvey Oswald, though in build I was more like Oswald than Robinson, who had the heavy set of Jack Ruby. I would go in like a two-gun cowboy, the little camcorder in my left hand to catch his face at the moment of impact, pistol in the right. The path of the bullet as it punched its way through his stomach would expel the air from his lungs, giving him Oswald's look of surprise.

I saw him again on the stern of a party boat as it passed Charing Cross. Like me he had lost weight. He was still stout, but he looked clean of drugs. He stood taller than the rest. The crowd on the river bank waved as the boat went by. The guests were society and sur-rounded by photographers. Robinson, dressed smartly in a plaid jacket, raised his hand in general salute to the shore. He was smiling and looked happy.

The riverboat party featured in the next day's evening paper, complete with photograph showing one shoulder of Robinson's jacket at the edge of frame. Every night there was one of these river parties, and most nights Robinson would be there. Though he never appeared fully in any of the photographs it was easy enough to monitor his progress: the back of his head in one; his out-of-focus face in another.

A big fancy dress party was announced, and received several days' advance publicity. It would be accom-panied by a large firework display, another indication of the mood of reckless celebration in the air.

I went dressed as Cookie, which I thought a neat touch. In tattersall waistcoat, tweed jacket and racing trilby I hardly passed for fancy dress, was, in fact, wearing what many of them wore for normal. The quayside looked more like Venice with people dressed as harlequins, skeletons, cardinals, Nell Gwynns. I hadn't counted on everyone wearing masks. Security was tight too. At the end of each gangplank a couple of bouncers checked invitations.

Robinson resisted this finale. He never showed up and I was left to imagine the ending to our film: a set-piece in which I stalked him through the party, trying to find the right Robinson because of everyone in fancy dress. Robinson, I believed, still kept many different personalities in his wardrobe, and, here, an actor to the last, he was caught in the hall of mirrors of his own magnificent vanity, in a room where, whichever way he turned, he was met by his own image.

The rains started again, and the electricity went off at the factory, ending all further work. The film – so close to perfection – suddenly lay in ruins. I moved, for the last time, to the house in St John's Wood, to wait for both of them. I took with me what equipment I could manage, using a discarded supermarket trolley to push it from Clerkenwell to St John's Wood, the wheels making little waves in the water.

The house was still connected to the mains. Television reported nothing but disasters and evacuations. One channel stopped broadcasting anything except old cartoons, and I wondered if it was evidence of a military coup. I taped more material to add to our project. Even on television there was a feeling that things were nearing their end. A newscaster broke down and wept.

I took our project apart and started again, seeing at

last how it had to go, the logic of each cut not only in re-
lation to the one before and the one after, but every
other cut, so that the film would cease to become linear
and sequential and the images would transcend their
assembled order to become simultaneous. Our film
would run in space, not time.

All it needs is for him to come. To see it, to give himself to its end. He'll come soon. I'm sure.

*I imagine him, his empire in ruins, and the deluge
already begun.*

*I see us playing out our last act on a barge in the basin
of Little Venice. Me filming Robinson engineering his
own destruction. The slash of the razor blade, the clean
cut, the unblinking gaze of curiosity. Watching his shoes
filling with blood, his slit wrist waxy, hanging over the
shoes as they fill. The only important thing, says Robinson, is the myth one invents for oneself.*

Robinson will make sure I am his witness.

*And the rain falls, and when I look out the sky is
ablaze and a convoy of planes drones overhead, and the
barge slips its moorings (or does Robinson order me, a
final request?) and we move from the basin down the
canal. This catafalque bears Robinson to the river that
has risen to meet us. The boat drifts between the drowning houses of Soho, and we pass that way one last time;
overhead a forked red sky. Then the whole raft of Soho
breaking from the rest of the city, and the smoke and the
fire. Robinson, 'the dirty rover of Oxford Street', gone in
the rupture. And gradually the shades come out, the
spirits of the place – the immigrants of the nights – and
the district moves like a huge, nearly submerged island
down into the swirl of the river's midstream, and then
seawards, past what was once Tilbury. Then the shades
are released and float into the black sky until only*

Robinson and I are left.

The toe-caps of Robinson's shoes are opaque now, as filmed as his eyes. Rough seas ahead, the waves starting to crest, one larger than the rest crashes down on to the bow. Somewhere, nearly lost on the wind, the mournful boom of a fog horn, a sign to release him to the waves. Robinson's white arm held aloft, as though in valediction, the last I see of him until the green swallows him.

Come away now.